Walk With
the Sickle Moon

Walk With the Sickle Moon

Helen Norris

A Birch Lane Press Book
PUBLISHED BY CAROL PUBLISHING GROUP

A Birch Lane Press Book
Published by Carol Publishing Group

Editorial Offices
600 Madison Avenue
New York, NY 10022

Sales & Distribution Offices
120 Enterprise Avenue
Secaucus, NJ 07094

In Canada: Musson Book Company
A division of General Publishing Co. Limited
Don Mills, Ontario

Manufactured in the United States of America

Library of Congress Cataloging-in-Publication Data

Norris, Helen, 1916-
     Walk with the sickle moon / Helen Norris.
          p.   cm.
     ISBN 1-55972-026-3 : $15.95
     I. Title.
     PS3527.0497W34   1989
     813'.52--dc20   89-7382
                                                CIP

For Mickey

Twist the old moon into the sickle.
Double-edged is the nursling moon.
Walk with the whetted moon, take care:
A dream in autumn is deadly fair
And the sweet child moon is keen to snare
And reap the cry of the loon.

I

WHEN Laura Kendall arrived in Montreuil, it was late September. And it was raining. Water was blowing from the high-pitched roofs and puddling among the cobblestones in the great open square. Transferring her from train to car, and in another moment from car to hotel, had not been simple. There was quite a ceremony of umbrellas and sharp calls, a profusion of offered arms, and gestures of support with words she could not understand. Rain brings out the chivalry in men. Especially, she thought she had observed, in Frenchmen. Though she was unknown to them, it made her feel announced and planned for.

Yet this was not what she had wanted. She had thought of slipping quietly inside the little city, of finding herself there almost as if by chance; so that if she could not face things after all, she could slip out unnoticed. And perhaps it would begin to seem as if she had not come.

When she signed her name at the desk, she felt a sudden wave of disquiet, because she did not really understand where she was. In a northern tip of France thrust into the Channel,

1

west of Flanders, southwest of Dunkerque. They were the only names that spoke to an American who could not call herself a tourist.

The clerk was reminiscent of all the dark young men that haunted hotel lobbies leaning over her name. "Madame Kendall," he said, pronouncing it so strangely that she thought at first he spoke of someone else. But he was smiling at her.

Indeed, he looked at her so graciously that on an impulse she decided to ask him a question, which the maps that she had studied on the train had left obscure. "Is this the province of Picardy?"

He shook his head. "Artois." He sounded reproachful.

She had hoped it might be Picardy, which she had heard of before. There was a song . . .

She wanted to ask him to repeat the name, but she lacked the courage. With a swift and practiced gesture, he passed the key to the elderly porter who brooded over her bag.

On the way up the stairs, to reassure herself, she turned and looked back at the neat, rustic lobby, the usual palms, the usual group of chairs before the unlighted fire. But a small panic seized her, because, quite profoundly, she did not know where she was. Oh, she knew it was a place; she could touch it on the map, buy a ticket, arrive. But she only began to understand why she had come.

Perhaps it was only that in all these years she had never seen herself arriving. She had not thought of the hotel.

She had not seen this room . . .

When the porter had left her, she took off her shoes and lay down on the bed, her eyes on the ceiling. She lay without moving. Outside, the wind heaped the rain against her window. After a while, she reached to turn off the light by the bed, which the porter had left on. And then, though it was afternoon, the room was gray as dusk. And like winter, she thought. Like winter . . . And she shuddered . . . Like the long, gray war which had clouded this land and even now shadowed the years that followed. Nine gray years they were calling peace . . . Was the shadow her own?

For a long, long moment, she did not know if she were going to unpack. She remembered, with the logic of a woman, and to put away her other reasons, that in less than a week she would have a birthday. She was not sure that she could bear becoming forty-five in this room . . . though it was nice, rather elegant in an understated way.

She listened to the rain. She lifted her hand and felt the skin of her face and her throat. And after all, what did it matter? It would be good to be quite old and look back, as from a distance, as if she were another person, on Laura Kendall, who had lost her son and then her husband and then had gone to Europe and become forty-five. Perhaps, when she was old enough, it would all run together, and the two griefs and the trip and the birthday would have for her the same sad remoteness . . . would be one rounded memory with no edges in between. No sequence. No crying out inside herself, "This happened. And then this happened . . ." Until she stifled it and cried instead, "What comes next?"

"What comes next?" she whispered now quite coldly and deliberately. And then she let herself remember why it was she was here.

She sat up at once and switched on the light by the bed. Her purse lay on the dresser. She walked across the room for it. And standing in her stockinged feet, she rummaged for the paperback guide book prepared for the American tourist, which she had purchased in Paris. Somewhere, perhaps in Italy, it had lost its cover. Although it was a guide to France alone, she had never packed it away, but had kept it in her handbag for the whole of the trip; as if she might at any time have left the party of eager sightseers and returned straightway to France. She had not quite had the courage. Once in Florence, she had almost slipped away. And again in Vienna . . . But the Tour was so fixed. It had a Will of its own. When destiny has humbled you, when you have lost your way in life, you find you do not have sufficient courage to defy the Tour.

She had allowed herself to be borne along and finally dropped in Paris where it came to an end. Then she had breathed deeply, free of its oppression, and had walked the streets around her hotel, losing herself in alien crowds, peering into shop windows and trying not to think. Putting off the question that always lay along the floor of her mind, "What comes next?"

But one day she asked it. And then she asked the hotel for a schedule of trains. And she came to Montreuil . . .

She sat down on the bed with the book in her hand and found the place. She kept her finger on the line while she picked up the phone.

The clerk answered her in something French, which she did not understand. Resolutely, she began in her best State of Virginia American: "This is Mrs. Kendall. I should like a little information."

"*Oui*, madame."

"There is a Cistercian chapel near by. About six miles, I think. The guide book I am using lists it with the Abbaye de Valloire."

There was a hesitation at the desk. She thought perhaps she had not pronounced the name correctly. She was beginning to spell it aloud, when he interrupted.

"*Oui*, madame. The Abbaye."

"I should like to see the chapel while I'm here. Could you tell me how I might arrange to do this?"

"*Oui. Oui.* Madame wishes to go to the Abbaye."

4

She waited for the slightest moment. "The chapel," she corrected.

"*Oui*, the chapel . . ." He broke off suddenly and spoke in rapid French to someone close at hand. She caught the sound of her name. "*Oui*, madame," he said again. "It will be necessary that madame rent the car at the garage."

She hesitated. "There is no one who could drive me?"

"I will call the garage for madame. I will ask if there is some one. It will depend . . ."

"On what will it depend?" she asked, her voice patient but weary. It had come to seem that everything in Europe depended on the tip. There was a price for things and for persons. And sometimes she confused the two. She paid the price for the thing at the moment that she should have paid the price for the person; and again, she would reverse the error. But perhaps it was a matter of the language. She could never be sure.

"It will depend, madame," he repeated. "Shall I call back, madame, when I have spoken with the garage?"

"Please," she said, and hung up.

She waited for a moment, her eyes closed. Then she got up and opened her suitcase and glanced at the clothes that she was sick to death of taking out and hanging up and putting back again. They had a damp, crestfallen look. But they belonged to the Tour, and as such they kept a little of its false, enthusiastic air; a little of its frantic now-or-never dash for culture, as if culture were a frontier they must cross before five. The tyranny of every schedule and the charm of every scene. And the comradeship! The way it was always: Laura, we found the shops. They have coral . . . they have leather . . . they have adorable figurines . . . well, they mail it for you, darling. I bought a chandelier. And the way it was always: Laura, wherever did you go? Why, we looked and couldn't find you, you missed that interesting old guide . . . well, he climbed us to

5

the top, such a view, you missed it . . . when her spirit wanted solitude, a little quiet dark peaceful place for a day, where there was nothing to climb or see or hear explained in bad English.

But after all she had deceived them. It was really her fault. She had not wanted the Tour, so she never found its spirit. She had tried, but not much.

She took out only her house slippers and put them on, and let the lid of the suitcase fall shut again.

Then she walked to the dresser. She studied herself critically, reluctantly, in the mirror. She had once been thought handsome.

There had been a year, just after she was married, before Jamie was born, that she had found herself so. But everything that year, including Laura Kendall, had seemed possessed of beauty. There was nothing really wrong with the look of her now. She might be taken for forty, a woman past her youth, who had her "pretty" days. Coming in from a walk, if she had not grown tired, if she had slept the night before and eaten her breakfast and failed to think about the past, and her hair had just been done—if all these things were so, she might catch a glimpse of herself and see that she was pretty. There were too many "if's." With every year that passed, another "if" was added. But with each passing year, she cared a little less.

There were wide-spaced eyes, an iris blue, that slanted faintly, striking a kind of angle with the shadows underneath. They were still her point of beauty, though they had grown a little weary, and the shadows underneath had plunged them into something like the color of evening. The mass of dark hair, only slightly touched with gray, with much time and effort she tamed to smooth waves, warring always with its tendency to spring into curls.

She took a comb from her purse and drew it slowly through her hair. She was thinking that they had not called her back about a driver. But it did not really matter. She was too tired to care. She had not slept well for nights. And on the train, in her compartment, two women had talked endlessly, endlessly in French. When you did not understand a word, at first it was restful. But after a while you fought it, to believe in yourself. To be sure you were there.

She walked to the telephone and picked it up.

"Could I have a little supper in my room?" she inquired. She listened for a moment.

"Anything that's on the menu," she replied. "I really don't care."

There was a silence. She had shocked him, of course. If you were French and you were dying, you selected your last broth. Or you carefully put yourself into the hands of one who would. If she had left it up to him . . . But she had said she didn't care.

"Whatever it is," she added bravely, "could I have it at seven?" She hung up. She had shocked him again. In France, she had decided, food existed out of time. For good food, you waited. The better, the longer; as a matter of course.

She went into the bathroom and began to draw a bath.

SHE WENT down for breakfast quite early the next day. The dining room beyond the lobby was a pleasing rustic room with a fine, large fireplace. The logs were freshly lighted. Bits of old glass and pewter on the mantel and in the corners reflected the flames. Beyond the window a formal garden was on fire with autumn. She ate her breakfast slowly, not wanting to leave. Outside lay a world that she could wait to encounter, that was whipped about with wind. It was good to sit quietly

7

between the fire in the room and the flame among the trees. It warmed and diverted her. The patch of sky that she could see had a tender, muted pallor, clean-washed and damp. The day itself seemed to spring from the garden underneath.

A melancholy waiter, with a single lock of hair brushed straight across his head, brought her coffee with milk and a plate of rolls. The coffee was very strong and bitter with chicory. "Would it be possible to have a little more milk with the coffee? Or some cream?" she asked.

He looked at her sadly and bowed and went away. He was limping a little. He remained away for some time; perhaps, she thought, to show that she had gone against the custom.

When at last he returned with milk, she asked about the weather. "Will it be a good day, do you think? Will the sun be coming out?"

He gazed through the window. "Ah, madame, the sun is out!" He said it reproachfully, and she looked again at the sky. It held a pale lemon light. A fragile, porcelain glow. But the sun . . . She could not find the sun at all.

She glanced at him, surprised. Perhaps it was the language. She could never be sure.

He disappeared again, and she returned to her coffee. The room, with several diners, had a kind of muted elegance. Life was suspended. The silver faintly sounded, but she had to be alert for it. A voice was barely separate from the rustle of the fire. In America, one felt the pressure of the lives of diners all around one, like an atmosphere of brave intentions. All the things that were intended when the eating was over. But here— she looked around her—nothing was intended. There was no future in the room.

But she faced it: I am making up a reason for remaining . . .

In the corner a lone gentleman, quite elderly, was reading the paper. It trembled not unpleasantly in his palsied hand. Not far from him, two ladies, brisk of manner but declining in years, were silently communing with their buttered rolls. And at the next table, but almost behind her so that she had to turn very slightly to see, sat a woman past her prime, gray-haired, gray-suited, ruddy-cheeked, with a vigorous, healthy presence that was not to be dispelled by her being out of sight. She seemed quite impervious to the room's quiet charm. But she was here; she belonged. Laura felt that she had sat here perhaps for years. She was at home with her table, its angle and its view.

Laura turned her back and took a sip of her coffee. But she felt the eyes of the other on her back, a scrutiny that teemed with speculation and logic and inherent disapproval of unreasonable missions. She speaks English, Laura sensed but without surprise. And in a moment she thought: She speaks it because she is English, herself. After all, we are not so very far from the Channel.

She felt a little glow of warmth about their common tongue. It gave her almost the lift she needed to be on her way. And at the same time, with those eyes upon her, she had never felt so strongly the unreality of her plan, of her being here at all.

She stood up quickly, while she yet had the heart. And the waiter was abruptly beside her with the bill. While she settled it, she caught the eyes of her neighbor, who was somberly smoking. And when they were alone, "Good morning," said the lady, with eyes half closed against the cloud she was producing. "I couldn't help overhearing that you asked about the weather. If you're planning a little trip, I would strongly suggest a topcoat. And a raincoat as well. You really can have no idea of the wind and the rain." She had a guttural but rather musical voice.

"Thank you," Laura said.

"And a hat that won't blow off. I have a special hat that I

9

wear in Montreuil. Every year, you understand, the very same hat. They were always blowing off. I got tired of tipping the natives who retrieved them."

Laura looked at her just-under-portly figure, at her warlike features, and the pink, flushed cheeks traced with tiny veins. She might have come in from a walk across the heath. If this were England, of course.

"You are American?" the lady asked.

"I'm afraid it shows," Laura answered.

"It does," she said firmly. And presently she added, "I'm Stella Carstairs. From across the Channel."

"And I'm Laura Kendall. It is comforting to find someone here who speaks my language. I don't know French at all."

"A miserable language." She stated it without emotion, as if it had been settled once for all long ago.

Laura laughed a little. "Well, of course it's hard to understand why everyone won't speak English." She was wondering if she heard the sound of rain against the window.

"They will come to it in time. French, we're always told, has been the language of diplomacy. But diplomacy is dead." She studied Laura through a curl of smoke. "And the dead don't speak." There was something half complacent, half embattled in her manner; and a curious disregard of the charm of her surroundings.

Laura smiled lightly and looked into the fire. "I suppose we shan't mind their keeping on with it for practical purposes."

The Englishwoman made an indefinable sound. "With the French," she observed, with meaning, "every purpose is practical."

Laura glanced at her doubtfully. After a moment she asked, "Is it Mrs. Carstairs?"

"My husband was Major Henry Carstairs, retired Army." She leaned back as if he had bequeathed her his authority.

"Every afternoon at four in my room I make tea. They will make it for you, yes, but it's abominably done. Mrs. Kermit often joins me. And Mrs. Spence, when she is here."

"Thank you," Laura said. "My plans are quite uncertain, but if I'm here I should like it."

"Then I'll expect you at four. If your plans will permit." She scrutinized Laura. You are staying for a while?"

"It will depend . . ." Laura said.

"I see. Upon your plans. Well, well, I won't keep you. But don't expect to see the sun. It never actually appears. I overheard the waiter. When it isn't really pouring, they say the sun is out."

"How odd! But never?"

"Never. I have looked for it for years. Sometimes of course you see the place where it would be if it would be. But it never quite erupts."

"How interesting!"

"But depressing."

"I see the point. Goodbye."

Laura left the room, conscious of the eyes on her back. She bore with her an impression of good will and bad humor, stirred and mellowed to a pungent mixture that she could not really say if she liked or if she disliked.

At the desk, she asked again about the car.

The clerk picked up the telephone. "Which machine would be pleasing to madame?"

"Something not too difficult for an American to drive. But I was hoping for a driver."

"Ah, *oui*." He spoke into the phone and paused. There began in a moment a rather lengthy conversation. He kept his eyes upon her. She had an uneasy feeling that she was being described, her probable abilities, her possible way with a machine . . .

11

He hung up at last. "Madame, they are sending for you the little Dauphine. In one moment it arrives. If madame will sit down . . ."

It failed to arrive for at least another hour. And she found it driverless. But the delay had given her time to study for the hundredth time a small map of the region which she kept in her purse; and to read again in her guide book: "The chapel is worth seeing, and is open to tourists. The Abbaye itself, where the monks of the Cistercian Order formerly dwelt, is situated, as was customary, between the forest and the river, an arrangement which made available both fuel and water. In recent years, it has been converted to an orphanage maintained by the Government. Not open to the public."

Not open to the public . . . She drove quite slowly over the rough cobblestones, to get the feel of the car. The huge town square was almost deserted. The wind swept through it and rocked the small car and whistled overhead. She passed the open galleries that lined the square. The stores behind them huddled, looking sealed against the wind. Here and there a pigeon started up from her path. And soon she was passing between the ancient, cone-shaped towers of the entrance to the town and going sharply downward and into the country on an asphalt road.

She had unfolded the small map and placed it beside her. And now she glanced at it quickly and back to the road.

Beside her were yellow willows and flamelike poplars tossing in the wind. And beyond stretched endless, stubbled, amber fields, dotted everywhere with stacks of wheat that were shaped like the towers she had left behind, but sturdy and low. She passed an occasional white-washed house, low-lying, with a steep-pitched orange roof that seemed, from the road, to be made of tile. All the shutters, she observed, were striped green and white. At length she noticed that the doors were striped too, and that each house, oddly, was bordered at the base with a band of black.

But she did not travel with a tourist's eye. Details that she might have found picturesque now moved her to caution and a deep unease. She did not today want the strange and unusual. She wanted to feel that she belonged to be here. And alien things in the country around her sounded inside her a vague alarm. She kept her eyes then on the asphalt road, which was like all the roads she had ever known.

Now that she was nearing the end of her journey—no, more than that; the end of seven years, since Jamie had died—she felt within her a deep reluctance. If the end should be other than she had dreamed . . . And suddenly, without warning, she faced it. She was frightened. And she almost whispered it: Why am I here?

She slowed her speed and glanced at the map, which showed a turn to the left. She drew to a stop, afraid that she had missed it. Around her the fields had altered to green. A truck was moving in the distance through the long, even rows.

Then, not far away, she saw the turn. She started toward it and turned from the highway down a narrow paved road. She was going downhill. The wind was at her back. Beef cattle grazed beneath shimmering elms. Damp golden leaves struck the windshield of the car. And beyond were the fields of deep green again. A wagon was approaching, drawn by heavy horses, and she pulled to one side to allow it to pass.

The driver was perched on a heap of white fruit or vegetables unfamiliar to her, his head bowed low into the oncoming wind, his cap pulled tightly down on his face, his legs dangling over the front of the cart. When the load passed, swaying, a bit of it fell and struck the hood of her car, and bounced and spattered on the road between.

In a moment, the whole of it had thundered past. She drew

her eyes back into the road and gathered speed. There was a
fine mist of rain forming on her windshield. In the distance,
the sky was looming heavy and low. She wanted all at once to
be done with the trip, to be there, to know . . .

Suddenly the car went out of control. It skidded on the
pavement, till it turned half around, nosing into the ditch. It
came to rest beneath a crouching willow, which showered its
yellow pointed leaves on the hood.

She got out slowly. She was a little dazed, but the cold
revived her. She did not seem to be hurt. But the car, she
decided, was hopelessly stuck. In the misting rain, she exam-
ined the front wheel sunk into the earth. Merely as a gesture,
she got in and spun the tires for a moment. Then she climbed
back out and looked around her. She had taken the raincoat
Mrs. Carstairs had advised. And now she put it on.

In the field ahead, and not far away, she saw a small white
farmhouse with a dark thatched roof that looked to have a
border of the orange tiles. She took off her hat and threw it
onto the seat and wound a scarf from the pocket of her coat
about her head. Then she got her purse and the keys from the
car and carefully climbed through the barbed wire fence,
which the willow had concealed. She found herself walking
between even rows of the strange green crop she had noticed
from the road, and the dark soil was caking on her fragile
shoes.

She looked up at the house ahead. There was no one around.
But above the striped door was a large white birdhouse. And as
she was seeing it, a bird flew into it. She stood quite still. She
did not know why, except that suddenly it seemed like a
strange kind of dream: her being here now on the eve of winter
in the north of France; her walking through the field slowly
and carefully in the too narrow space between the dark green
rows; and the bird flying into the house of its own, so swiftly

14

and surely that it seemed to fly through into the larger house. She could see it in her mind circling inside beneath the dark, thatched roof . . . striking its head against the small shuttered windows. And she whispered it at last, "Why am I here?" in a wild kind of panic that was like the bird's and a blind rush of yearning for her distant land.

A voice called, "*Allo,*" and she turned around quickly. The wind blew the end of the scarf against her eyes. When she took it away, she saw a man approaching through the field from the road. A sturdy figure in a brown trench coat. His head was bare. The wind was whipping through the ends of his cropped gray hair. Then she saw the car parked on the road beside her own.

He came closer and stopped at some distance away. "It is your car, madame?" he asked against the wind. He spoke with an accent.

"Yes," she answered, her heart still.

"I am Marc Duriez."

She was so relieved that he had come and could speak her language that she almost stumbled.

"Madame?" he said, moving closer. "You were hurt, is it so? I am a doctor."

"No, no, I'm all right. But I am so glad to see you."

The wind blew his open trench coat about him. He was watching her gravely. There were lines raying out from his steady gray eyes.

She said to him, "I could not think what to do." It relieved her to see that he was older than herself, if only by a little. There had become too many people in the world who were younger and suspected her of being more foolish than she was. At this moment, she was fighting for a meager self-respect.

She began in apology, "I can't think how it happened. The car very suddenly went out of control . . ."

15

"You slipped on the beets . . . But they are very dangerous." He said the last word awkwardly, though she quite
understood it. But the other . . . She inquired, again with
apology, "What was it you said first?"

"You slipped on the beets. It is the beetroot. For sugar." He
waved his hands at the rows of green at their feet. "In this time
of the harvest the road is difficult for travel. They fall, these
beets, from the wagons and the trucks to the pavement and
. . ." He stopped and gestured. He could not think of the
word. "On the pavement they are like . . ." He narrowed his
eyes and shook his head. He smiled. "They are placing you in
the ditch in one moment."

She nodded quickly. "That is just what happened."

He looked past her to the house. "You were going for
help?"

"Yes," she said. "To this house."

"It is of no benefit. It is the house of a very old woman and
her son. He would be away with the beets in the truck at this
hour."

"Then I am very fortunate . . ."

"We shall return to the car?" he interrupted.

She nodded again.

They began to walk back through separate paths between
rows. She saw him glance down at her mud-caked shoes. In a
moment, he was helping her through the fence.

When they reached the road, he circled her car, disappearing
for a moment beneath the willow. Emerging, his eyes on the
sunken wheel, he said to her, abstracted, "The key, if you
please." And when she handed it to him, "You will wait in my
car."

She turned obediently.

"One moment," he said, and preceded her to fetch a cloth
from the rear. "For the shoes," he said bluntly and handed it to

16

her, his eyes on her car. Then he stooped and picked up a rock
in each gloved hand from the marshy earth and walked away.

She got into his car and took off her shoes and cleaned them
while she held them at arm's length through the window. They
looked better than she had feared, and she put them on. Then
she combed her hair carefully before the rear-view mirror and
powdered her face. She was beginning to feel cold. But at once
she heard the motor and saw her car backing from the ditch
into the road.

She got out to meet him, her hair blowing wildly in the wind
again. "How can I thank you!" she said, when he again stood
in the road.

"Madame will take care." He pointed to a white beet burst
open just ahead. "It is best to go slow and avoid." He turned to
her. "Madame is going to where . . . to what destination?"

She hesitated but a moment. "To see the chapel at the
Abbaye."

He bowed very slightly. "It is good. Than you shall go
before. I shall go behind."

She looked at him perplexed.

"It is the same destination. As is mine," he explained.

Still, she looked uncertain. "The chapel?" she asked.

"I go to the home for the children just beside."

After a moment she asked: "But how is it . . . I had thought
. . . I believe it isn't open to the public."

"I am the doctor for the children."

"I see. Of course."

Still, she stood in the road with her eyes upon him, as if she
wanted to ask more.

He held open her door. "Madame, you are American?" He
asked it, unsmiling.

But she smiled at him. "I suppose it is obvious." After a
pause she added, "I am Laura Kendall."

17

He looked at her, expressionless, his face remote and listening. Then he bowed and turned away. Perhaps, she thought, he does not care for Americans. She was truly sorry. But to his gesture of assistance it gave a touch of real charity . . . In a moment she heard his motor, and she started hers.

The misting had stopped. Ahead in the sky she saw a delicate light. There was a faint smell of smoke and a smell of the sea. She drove quite slowly, aware of his car in the rearview mirror. With the shock of it over, she began to feel foolish about her trouble on the road. A small, delayed tremor crept into her throat. So near the end of her journey, she had gathered herself together, drawn tense and expectant. And anything, the least thing, was enough to make her shatter.

"I don't shatter," she said aloud. "I have lived through more than this." In a moment she must appear to be serene and self-possessed. She must inspire confidence. She must seem to be a kindly, calm American woman.

But not too American . . . American blood and French sympathies, she must have, she thought grimly. Really, a French heart in an American breast. She shook her head slowly in a richness of despair, till she saw the doctor's car in the mirror again. And for one intense moment she thought of telling him her mission, perhaps enlisting his help.

But he had looked so reasonable. And after all, she was afraid of the reasonable mind's reaction to what she proposed. She was afraid of herself . . . that if she were led to see it in the cold, clear light of reason, she would turn aside.

She was traveling downhill, and the wind was subsiding. There was a wood on the right. The land rose behind it in a sweep of russet hills. Before her was a green-silver smoke of firs. At once she had arrived. She saw the iron-work gate; and beyond it, the courtyard and the Abbaye itself of grayish white stone, rather fine and imposing, as she had seen it in the books, with a rustic kind of elegance. Then her heart contracted with the thought that she was here, at the end; and that after this . . . after this, there was nothing else.

She parked beside the road. And while she waited for Dr. Duriez to pull up beside her, she combed her hair again and put on her hat, a tight little felt which almost hid the fact that her waves, in wind and dampness, had reverted to curls. A short man in a beret was opening the gate. The doctor sped past her into the courtyard, beckoning her to follow. In a moment, she had done so. Then she stepped quickly to the cobbled pavement. She looked again at the Abbaye and was suddenly overwhelmed at her own strange folly.

She saw the doctor approaching. He had taken her hesitation for uncertainty about the chapel. "Madame," he said, "through the door of the Abbaye, it is the way to the chapel."

She nodded. "Shall I go in with you?"

"If you will, please, I will show it."

On either side were low buildings, and before her the main, storied wing of the Abbaye. She stood with deep reluctance, and yet with eagerness, unable to move. She saw that he was watching. Her eyes swept the ivied stone, the handsome iron grillwork of the long, low windows, and the gray double doors.

"It is so much like the pictures," she said quietly, because he seemed to question.

And suddenly from a gable window on the third floor above, a child was looking out at them. Her heart stood still. She turned away, her eyes blind. "Will you show me where to go?"

"But of course. We shall go in."

They went up the steps and through the large double doors. She had not foreseen the stillness. It startled her a little. Nor the sound of a typewriter. That, too, was strange. He stopped before a doorway through which it seemed to be coming; and turning to her, he inclined his head a little.

"Madame, the chapel is before, at the end of the corridor."

"I see," she said. "And thank you. You have been more than kind . . . more than kind." She wanted to say something else, but in these surroundings she was oppressed and at a loss. She had dreamed of them for months. She had seen herself standing in a corridor like this . . .

He made a gesture with his hand. "But no, madame." He turned into the doorway, and she heard a woman greeting him in French in a deep, assured voice.

She walked on slowly, looking up and down the hall. No one was in sight. Up the stairs and at a distance, she heard a rhythmic buzz of high voices, as if a poem were being said in unison. She paused to listen. The voices stopped abruptly. And then quite close at hand, at the head of the stairs, a woman spoke with authority. *"Non, non, non. Ah . . . oui."*

She walked the length of the hall. And at the end, on the left, were massive doors of oak. She stood before them pretending to be engrossed in her guide book. And presently she heard the doctor leave and mount the stairs and walk down a hall above. In a moment, his footsteps sounded overhead.

She turned abruptly and retraced her steps. She paused only briefly outside the doorway he had left. Then she entered quickly. There was no one about. It was a small, narrow room with several chairs against the wall. She stood there uncertainly. Presently, behind the wall, a chair was pushed back and some one came toward her. She was greeted in French by a tall, comely woman slightly younger than herself, severely, darkly dressed.

Laura smiled and said easily. "I am Laura Kendall. I speak only English." She had rehearsed it many times.

The woman scanned her swiftly.

"I am American."

"Yes," said the woman. Then she added clearly in accented English, "The chapel is at the end of the corridor. The door at the end."

Her English had a practiced, automatic fluency. Laura heard it with relief. It struck her now how much she had relied on this fluency. She smiled again. "I did not come to see the chapel. I came to ask your help." She looked around her. "I wonder if I may sit down and explain." She had tried to keep the tenseness from her voice, to seem assured and at ease. But scanning the woman's face, she caught the curious, guarded look.

Laura asked, "You are in charge . . . of the orphanage?"

"I am *la directrice*."

". . . Then may I ask your help?"

The woman turned her head slightly. "Come in here," she offered. She led the way into the farther room, a well-appointed office. Two windows, long and grilled, reached almost to the floor. "The chair, if you please." She waved her hand in its direction.

She sat behind the desk, and at once she had been braced for the improbable request that was impossible to grant. The lines of her mouth began to shape a courteous refusal. Her eyes were pleasant but opaque and impervious to appeal. And Laura saw that, after she herself had spoken for five minutes, the face would not have changed. She dropped her eyes. She reminded herself that, more or less desperately, she had wanted this moment for two years—no, surely since Jamie had died and that was longer, that was seven years . . . She must by some word change the face before her.

She began to speak. "My son died in France. I have reason to believe that his child may be here." She could say it quite well, because she had said it to herself so many times in the past months. It was almost like a play for which she had rehearsed. Indeed, she was suddenly struck with the unreality of the scene, as if she had dreamed it and were dreaming it again.

The face before her gave no sign. She went on. "He had been serving his year with the army. I believe he was in Paris most of the time. And then . . . just before he was to come home . . . he was killed in an accident. The car . . . he was thrown." She paused for a moment to look around the room. "They sent his things. Everything that was his. It is customary, I believe, to send the personal effects. And in his wallet I found a note from a girl. It was written in French. Her last name was not given, but it came from this region. It was postmarked at Montreuil."

"Montreuil," said the director, as if it were the one thing on which they possibly agreed.

"Yes, Montreuil," Laura answered. She had practiced the name in order to say it correctly. She looked at the metal cabinets behind the director's chair. Presently, without taking her eyes from them, she resumed, "In this letter, this note . . . it was very short . . . she said that she was having a child of my son's . . . I sent it to some one who translated it for me."

"Madame, you must understand that I have not the authority. I take the direction . . . You understand the Abbaye is under the direction of the government of France." In her clipped, accented words, the Abbaye sounded impregnable.

Laura turned her eyes upon her. "I am not asking you to let me take the child . . . I am only asking . . . I am asking if that child is here." The other was silent. "You have records . . ."

The director smiled firmly. "Madame, the records are the possession of the Government. I have not the permission . . ."

Laura looked at her for a long moment. "I had hoped

. . ." she began. She paused and started anew. "When I understood this note, its meaning . . . I found things to read about this region of France. And when I read about this orphanage, it seemed to me it might be here that the child would be. From the note, I believed she might not keep the child. It seemed to me I could not rest till I could come here and know."

"Madame, I regret."

Laura Kendall looked down at the hands in her lap. She saw that they were trembling. She said at last simply, "I have come a long way."

"Madame, you will understand I have not the authority." She rose and stood before the desk.

Laura did not look up. "May I tell you how it happens that I have the courage to be here? When it came, this letter, I did not tell my husband. He was ill . . . quite ill . . . His son's death had been a shock. I did not think I should tell him of the other . . . of the child in France. So I waited. And he never became well. He died three years later. And since then . . . I have come to know that I must find this child." After all, she could not put it into words.

"Madame . . ."

"I am not wealthy. But I am far from poor. There are things I could do . . . that I wish to do . . ." She broke off.

The director stood silently.

Laura Kendall rose. "Forgive me," she said quietly. She looked up into the eyes of the woman before her. "Perhaps, before I go, I could see the children."

The director closed her eyes, then shook her head. "They are in the classrooms."

"If I waited . . ."

"Madame . . . children are easily . . ." she sought the

word, "disturbed. I am responsible to see that it does not happen."

Laura looked at her silently, then nodded slightly. A moment later she found that she was walking down the hall. She meant to leave by the entrance and find her car. But looking up, she saw that she had reached again the massive double doors into the chapel.

She stood before them in a sudden blind surge of despair. I have done it all wrong, she was thinking. I have ruined it all. . . . And she seemed to see that somewhere in Paris she might have found the official who could open for her the records and the rooms overhead.

Dimly in the distance she heard a child reciting. She looked back, her eyes weary and bewildered; and down the hall a small girl in braids and a blue serge dress was leaning over the stairs, her cheek upon the rail, and watching her intently.

Laura turned away. The great entrance before her seemed locked and forbidding. Then she noticed that on either side were small swinging doors. She was suddenly very tired and she wanted to sit down. She passed through on the left and into the church.

Inside, it was so luminous and still that she waited, for a moment overwhelmed, her hand on the leather-covered door through which she entered. Then she went slowly forward through the vaulted space and dropped into one of the wooden chairs at the side. Before her was an intricate tracery of wrought iron; and beyond this, an altar and a great elaboration of figures and paneling.

On the Tour, she had tried to see interiors of churches with the eyes of her guide. Her own provincial eyes had brought her little understanding. Now she thought humbly, and with a kind of desperation of relief: I am finished with the Tour; as if only at this moment had she broken really free. She closed her eyes against the carving and the angels. She listened to the stillness. She smelled the ancient wood. And suddenly her mind was whispering. It always waited for the silence. "What comes next?"

To stop the sound of it, she opened her eyes wide on the vaulted ceiling. Beyond the lace-like gate, and high above the altar, two winged children hovered. She kept her eyes upon them; as if the sight of them, their bodies solid and unmistakable, hovering above this moment, could hold the future at bay.

But slowly, as it always did, the past crept behind her. Till in her mind she must at last turn and find it . . . and greet it. For it was what she had become. It was Laura Kendall.

This happened. And then this happened . . .

After Jamie had died, and she was left alone with Jim, she refused to acknowledge but that somehow . . . somewhere close at hand, Jamie *was*. There are three of us still, she had assured herself. And she kept on saying it, in the day and in the night.

After Jim died, she might have gone on saying, There are three of us still. But somehow it had come about that there was no one but herself. It had happened while she slept, and she had waked up and known it.

For many days, for months, there had been no one but herself . . . till slowly she grew aware that in the world there was another. Her own blood, her child's child. And her life had come to mean that she must find this child.

She drew her eyes from the ceiling and rested them on the black and white pattern of the floor. Near by her lay a black leather volume, perhaps a book of devotions. Its black marking ribbon lay outstretched on the floor. She looked at it for some time, seeing only how it cut across the pattern of the floor, and trying not to think, till vaguely it disturbed her to see how it lay, its ribbon flung aside and marking no page, as if there

25

were no passage one had wanted to recall. No phrase that spoke truth. No comforting word . . .

After a while, she leaned over and picked it up. And when she held it in her hand, she began to remember, with a strange lift of her heart, how when she was young, she and her sister used to play a sort of game that would tell the future. They would close their eyes tightly and, groping blindly, they would open the great Bible that lay always on the center table in the hall. Then running a finger down the unseen page, they would suddenly pause, and pointing firmly, breath held, they would open their eyes to read.

She went on holding it in her hands for a while, caressing the limp, cool leather with her palms. And at last she closed her eyes and opened the book.

When she looked again, she was staring at the strange, foreign words . . . Slowly she placed the marker on the page and enclosed it. She put the volume on the chair beside her. Her throat was dry. What comes next? She was thinking it all over again and staring through the delicate flowerlike gate, yet seeing nothing beyond. At last, she was a stranger in an alien land . . . homesick for the place where she had buried her dead.

Then she sat with a hand across her eyes, till she seemed to be drifting out of time and out of space. It was the way in which she had long since learned to cope with her grief. Some women thought of their childhood, she had heard, till they were children again . . . She knew that some quietly or desperately prayed. But for herself she had discovered this deliberate detachment. And then if she waited long enough, scarcely breathing, her eyes closed and looking neither outward nor inward, something . . . or someone always reached out to her in love. She sat tense and open. It was like the love of parents and husband and son . . . and like the love of a friend she had

had as a girl. It was all of these and more. More, more, she kept thinking. And then she must retreat from it, come back into herself; or slowly a new sorrow would creep into her heart. It seemed to spring from a knowledge that she could not love back. She could take this strange-familiar love till she was filled with it and warmed; but when she tried to return it, as deeply she longed to do, something held her, grief held her, and she could not break free. Or was it that a door had closed inside her forever.

Now she drew away her hand and opened her eyes. And it seemed to her at that moment that there had never been a child . . . She was thinking: If my son had had a child and that child were in this place, I would know it, I would feel it . . . There could not be any doubt.

There would be this one thing left in the dark that I could love . . .

She rose very quietly and went out of the chapel. In a moment, she found again that she had taken the wrong way, that she was in a walled garden. The hedges were clipped and glistening in the damp air. There were hardy chrysanthemums neatly tied, intensely brilliant, and a strong smell of earth.

Always, when loneliness possessed her for a time and drew a veil across her eyes, so that she scarcely saw the world, there would come a sudden reversal—in her eyes or in her heart, she could never be sure—and the world about her would be clothed in this strange, sharp brilliance, this freshness, this beauty . . . as if it cried out that she could never give it up.

As I can't, she thought humbly, leaning over a flower. She could feel it shudder through all its petals when she touched it. Or was it her own fingers? There was always in herself this little shiver, like a vibrating, indrawn breath, when she returned to herself, to the world, out of grief.

Abruptly she saw that she was not alone. An old man was

kneeling almost at her feet. He had a trowel in his hand, and he was watching her, faintly curious, with the eyes of a child.

"Good morning," she said, but she knew at once that he did not speak her language. She had become, in fact, intuitive in the matter, she had found. But now she did not care. "Your flowers are lovely." It made her feel oddly freer to be able to speak to him and not be understood.

He shook his head. A faint, rousing wind stirred the tips of the flowers.

"I know," she said, "I know. It doesn't matter at all." Suddenly they were smiling into one another's eyes. And in the midst of the smile, it seemed to her more than possible that the child was in this place.

She looked away and past the old man. There was a narrow grilled gate that opened out into the lawn and the trees. As if by some appointment with herself, the children ran past and called out to one another. They must have been dismissed while she was in the chapel. She stood in hope and wonder, and in fear. But this is given me, she thought. She walked around the old man and slowly toward the gate. When she reached it, they were gathering quite close at hand. And then began a running, chasing game. They tore past her so swiftly that she could scarcely see their faces. But presently they fell laughing in a heap on the grass, some rolling and some as still as if at once they fell asleep.

She stared at them, in turn, drawing each face deliberately down into herself. There was something in each . . . A mist came before her. For suddenly, unbelievably, they were all like her son . . .

She turned away and leaned against the gate. The old man was staring up at her as if she had alarmed him. She did not smile at him now. For a moment, she closed her eyes.

When she opened them, carefully she looked at the flowers.

28

A small bird, perhaps a thrush, was hopping under the hedge. And a pale yellow butterfly was alighting on the path. She looked again at the old man. His face was questioning hers. "My son was like my husband," she said to him and to herself, as if the words could measure the length and breadth of her loss.

She turned back to the children. They were lying still and tumbling as before. She studied them quite calmly, as if they might be children she had known all their lives, and now she was deciding what their faces would become. She tried to see them with love, and yet with not enough to blind her. She tried to find them strange, if indeed they were so.

And slowly it came about—it surprised her how completely—that in none of these faces did she find her son . . . She relaxed from the tension and dropped her head against the gate.

"Madame . . ."

She started and turned suddenly. Doctor Duriez was standing just behind her. She had not heard him coming, so absorbed she had been.

He was looking down at her with his detached and level gaze. "Madame, you are not well?"

"But of course. I'm quite well."

He hesitated. She felt her face begin to flush beneath his scrutiny. "You have completed the chapel?"

"Yes, I have finished with it, thank you."

He continued to look at her.

"It is quite beautiful," she said, for want of something to break the silence. "Most impressive, I thought." She added, "I'm sure I did not understand many things."

"I should be of little help."

"I did not mean to suggest . . ."

"Madame," he interrupted, "if you are ready, we shall go."

She looked at him, surprised.

He said, "It is well, since both are leaving, that I drive the road behind you."

"That is kind of you," she said, "but I am really quite well."

"Of course," he agreed. "But there will be the beets."

"Yes, the beets. How could I have forgotten! You are very, very kind."

When they turned to leave, she looked for the gardener, but he was nowhere around.

She drove with her window down. For as far as she could see, a strong wind was tearing at the stubble of the wheat. The sky was milk white, opaque with cloud. And it looked to be raining where the elms were huddled. The clear, rushing air had a smell of the sea. But now and then, before they reached Montreuil, there were apples in the wind like a high, sweet sound.

She could see the car behind her if she looked in the mirror, but when she neared the hotel, it had disappeared.

AT THE INN, they were in the dining room for lunch. But she did not feel hungry and went to her room. She lay down, and she was thinking that it was just as it had been the afternoon before, when she lay on her bed after entering this room; except that now she had done what she had come to do. She had gone, she had inquired, she had come away with nothing.

It was raining again. She could hear it at the window. And the wind was like a faraway, insistent voice. After a while, she heard the women padding up the stairs and down the hall to their rooms, to lie down after lunch. Then they were shut away in their separate lives, sealed off from one another in deliberate silence. A telephone rang, a bleating, frightened sound, and was abruptly stifled. The wind was coming closer and clutch-

30

ing at the panes. Finally, there was the rustle of steam in the pipes.

And at last she was thinking it: What comes next?

The past comes next. What else? What else?

But no, she protested, I will think about today. It had its humorous side, if she carefully looked. She had come all this way, she had survived the Tour. And then the beets and the ditch . . . She tried to see it as she might have seen it for Jim. And then she was thinking of the past, after all.

From the very beginning, between herself and Jim there had been a gay sort of thing. A little tender laughter at the core of their marriage, as if they shared a private joke that was good to remember. If things went well, the laugh was happy; if ill, it was rueful. But it was always their little secret that the humor was there and must be found and shared. It made a gallant kind of marriage. It was even like a race between the two of them sometimes to be the first to find the gaiety at the heart of their life . . . to hold it up and say, "Look . . ."

And it worked. It worked well, until the telegram came. Then their marriage seemed to stop. Like an engine that wouldn't run when the weather got cold. Or like a dream that faded when you finally woke. Or like a stream that stopped flowing when the spring dried up. They could not bear the betrayal in one another's eyes.

If they had only stood, the two of them, against the world, they could do so now. But they had always stood a little separate, tossing the glad secret back and forth to each other. If you stood too close you couldn't see to catch and pass it back. If you stood too close you'd miss the smile on the face of the other. There had to be the little distance . . . And now it widened.

She had held on, waiting . . . waiting for it to change; or waiting till she was strong enough to swim the distance. But

31

Jim went on retreating—or slowly died; it seemed the same—
until finally one morning he didn't wake up, he couldn't come
back. And the marriage was over.

She had wanted desperately to feel it wasn't over, that
something real remained. But she didn't, it was all. Jamie had
been the only fruit of their marriage, and the vine that had
produced him had died with him. And the knowledge of it gave
her a strange sort of guilt. Sometimes she was overcome with
guilty longing and wanted to reach out into the world and make
amends. To bring it close, to find in it something beyond the
gay, warm laughter, fine as it had been. To find the dark,
suffering heart of the world and make it hers.

It seemed to her a deep irony, almost like a joke she might
have shared with Jim, that on the threshold of middle age she
should discover in herself the reservoir of dark emotion, of
yearning, of compassion so overwhelming that at times she
was frightened . . . when now it was too late. When now she
should be drawing in her nets, however empty, and seeking a
little peace that she could lie with till the end.

She got up and walked around the room. She switched on
the light and sat in the flowered linen chair by the window and
tried to read a magazine she had bought in Paris. In the corner
of her eye, she could see the suitcase at the foot of her bed, still
packed with her clothes. And then quite suddenly she remembered Mrs. Carstairs' invitation to tea.

She was almost afraid to look at her watch . . . afraid it was
too late. She had an hour to spare.

Laura knocked on the door.

"Come in, my dear," said Mrs. Carstairs, when she opened
it, "and do sit down. And will you wait for one moment while
I finish with the young man."

Laura saw that a fair-haired boy, perhaps six or seven, was
sitting in the midst of a flowered linen chair like her own. Or

rather, on the edge, for his feet were dangling and his hands gripped the cushion. She hesitated. "Have I interrupted something? Let me come back later."

"Not at all. Not at all. It will be good for him to have an audience. Sit there," she said. She studied her watch. "We have ten minutes more."

She watched Laura sit. Then she sat down and sighed and put on her pink-rimmed glasses, which were hanging on her bosom by a silver chain. "This is Jean," she said to Laura. "Jean Duriez."

"Duriez?"

"Dr. Duriez's grandson."

Laura smiled. "I have met the doctor."

Mrs. Carstairs looked interested. "An estimable man. Well, this is his grandson. He has been taking English lessons from Mrs. Spence, who was staying here. Once a week, I believe. She had to leave suddenly. Her sister died." She stared across the rims of her glasses at the boy. "She left me this child . . . This is the last lesson. Jean, is this the last lesson?"

"Yes," said Jean.

"Yes, what?"

"Yes, Mrs. Carstairs."

"You see." She turned to Laura. "His accent is better than mine." She brooded for a moment. "In the depths of his soul I am still Madame Carstairs. Not that I mind. I think it has a certain elegance, don't you? But I was told to end it . . . It is a fact," she confided, "That the last time—I believe the only other time—I taught anyone to speak English was when I was in the mountains of Burma with the Major. I had three naked Indians, full-grown, male. And I taught them as a favor to the Major's commanding officer. They insisted upon reciting daily the parts of the body. It was all that seemed to interest them. Afterwards, I had a nervous breakdown. A total collapse . . .

Jean," she broke off, "is entering school next week. For the first time. That is why we can't continue these lessons . . . Jean, what day does school begin?"

"It begins on . . . Monday," he said slowly, darting a glance around the room that halted for a moment on Laura's face.

"What day will be your holiday?"

"Thursday," he said carefully.

"Ah, you see he knows his days." In the presence of the child, her warlike manner of the morning had shifted. She kept her weapons, but she aligned herself with him. "At what hour will you begin?"

"At the eight hour."

"Ah-ah-ah-h . . ."

"At eight o'clock."

"You see, he tells time. You can't imagine what a relief it is to teach a fully clothed being . . . Now, where is that picture? There is another picture for the lesson. There are two just alike. Jean, have you seen it?"

"The picture is beneath the chair of the woman." He said it carefully, distinctly, his eyes on the floor.

"Ah . . . there it is! You have very good eyes. Mrs. Kendall, would you reach it? It is under your chair."

Laura bent to pick it up. It was a colored print. It seemed to represent the members of a family having tea.

"Thank you. Now, Jean, will you take it from Mrs. Kendall?"

When he approached her, it struck Laura suddenly, as if it beat once against the wall of her mind, that the child she was seeking was the age of this child. And holding out the picture, her hand trembled a little. "How old are you, Jean?" She was surprised to hear her voice.

He looked into her face for a moment, then down at the picture. His eyes were quite blue. "I have seven years," he said. He was shy of her. His sturdy, rather square little face was slightly flushed.

"Ah-ah . . ." said Mrs. Carstairs.

"I am seven years old."

"That is better. Much better."

Laura drew in her breath. She was deeply, strangely certain that every child of this age would always haunt her a little. Even after years, she would give a second glance to every child who was seven, as if by some magic the one she once had sought at this time, in this place, had never grown any older.

She watched him turn and go back to his chair. And then she was aware that her thought had just acknowledged that she would leave here alone.

Mrs. Carstairs studied the picture, then the child, and again the picture. Her face was austere. "It is awkward," she said to Laura. "You never know how much they understand. An English child, for that matter, I never know how much he understands. But a French child, good heavens . . . And whatever it is he comprehends, does he do it by intuition or translation?"

"I see your point," Laura said.

"Young man," said Mrs. Carstairs, "do you understand my every word? Or do you put it all together and get a general idea?"

He looked at her steadily, his face very still, his chin slightly raised. He seemed curiously untouched, and yet alert to her strangeness.

"He doesn't know," said Mrs. Carstairs. "How could he possibly know? I wouldn't know, myself, if some one should ask me." She drew a handkerchief from the bosom of her blouse and blew her nose neatly. "This miserable climate! I feel I'm getting a chill. Now," she said smartly in a military tone, and lifted the picture. "Look at your picture, Jean."

He dropped his eyes to it obediently.

"Tell me what you see in the picture."

"It is a family," he began. "The baby is on the floor."

"And who is at the table?"

"The mother is at the table. And the father. And the boy. And the grandfather . . ."

"And who is in the rocker?"

"The moving chair?" he asked.

"Yes, yes."

"I do not know."

"Of course you do. Think who is missing."

"Is it the *grandmère* . . . grandmother?" he corrected it.

"Ah good . . . very good! You see he knows his relations. What color is her hair?"

"It is white," he replied.

"I understand his hesitation. She looks a little aged to be paired with the grandfather," she confided to Laura. "I think it is highly possible that he married her for money—the first husband's money—and they don't get on." She held the print at arm's length. "And the children look as if they had been left on the doorstep." She fixed Jean with her eye. "You see, he knows his colors . . . What is the color of your grandmother's hair?"

He regarded her silently, his eyes steady and alert. "I have not the grandmother," he said at last. His voice was patient.

"Ah, that is too bad. Too bad, too bad." She brooded over the picture. "They all look liverish," she observed with distaste.

Laura sat with a strange, dull ache in her heart. It was as if she heard, in the careful, halting words of the child, an echo of

36

the morning. Somewhere inside, she listened quietly, intently; not really to his words, but to the sound of his life, of his seven short years. As if they made a keen vibration in the air, which all morning long she had tuned herself to feel. She thought with a kind of wonder that she had never been so conscious of her son when he was little. Not acutely like this, with bone and with nerve.

She closed her eyes, and when she opened them, he was looking at her with interest.

Mrs. Carstairs blew her nose. Emerging from the handkerchief, she announced that they were finished. "I fail to see why we should waste good English on this unpleasant looking family." She creased them down the middle and pushed them under a cushion.

"Well, Jean," she said nasally, lost again in her handkerchief, "what is the good of knowing more? If you knew any more words, you would get into trouble. Of course Mrs. Spence has been paid by your grandfather to take an opposite approach. But since I haven't been paid, I am free to speak the truth. Words are overrated. My husband, Major Carstairs—the Major would have liked you—he used to say he went to India with half a dozen English words packed in his grip, and left ten years later with three of them still packed . . ." She studied him with speculation. "The three he used," she observed, her eyes narrowed on his face, "are ones that I trust you will never need to know."

She took off her glasses and let them tumble to her breast. She stood up stiffly. "Well, goodbye. And God bless you. I would say it to you in French, but the word for 'bless' I can't remember."

He got to his feet. His eyes were on her glasses, which were loose from their chain and were dangling precariously by a single earpiece.

"You tell me," she invited.

"*Dieu vous bénisse,*" he said low and clearly, looking down at his feet.

"Splendid!" she exclaimed. "I'm sure he says it better than the *curé*. I would shake hands," she announced, "if I didn't have a cold. But the doctor is too busy to have his grandson in bed."

"Now," she said, "goodbye again," and she put her hand on the door. "Don't forget to count to ten. And the days of the week. That is possibly all that you will ever need to know. Ah, put your jacket on now. Did you bring a raincoat? But I suppose the good grandfather will pick you up in the lobby."

He struggled into his jacket. Laura put out her hand to help him, but she drew it back.

"*Au revoir,*" said Mrs. Carstairs, still not opening the door. "Next year, Mrs. Spence may lose another of her sisters. They are all very frail. And then we shall take it up where we leave off now."

He glanced at them brightly, his face a little flushed. His collar was turned under. Then he looked at the door.

"Well, off with you." She flung it open, and he darted through.

She shut it slowly. "They always make me feel that I have cornered a bird. Charming child. Charming child. The Major would have liked him. And much like the doctor? Or wouldn't you agree?"

"Yes," said Laura, thinking, "I believe I would."

"Well, sit down, do. It is *Mrs.* Kendall?"

"Yes, it is," said Laura, seating herself again in her chair.

Mrs. Carstairs remained standing and lit a cigarette. "But traveling alone?"

"My husband is dead."

"But of course. It always shows. In the eyes, you know. As

if one had suddenly been dropped and didn't bounce. In the case of a divorce, they have always bounced. Not much, perhaps. But always to a degree. You must notice Mrs. Kermit if she comes for tea."

"She has bounced?" asked Laura.

"Rather high, rather high. Like a fresh tennis ball." She narrowed her eyes. "But I would say that perhaps she is losing it a little. Her altitude, I mean,"

She fetched a spirit lamp from the floor of the closet, and a small copper kettle, and disappeared with the latter into the bathroom. So prolonged was the splashing and the rinsing that Laura began to think that she was dressing for tea. At last, with the pale, severe brow of a priestess, she emerged with a teapot and the brimming kettle and began her ritual.

Laura sat watching her, wanting to be gone. The encounter with the child had stirred her deeply. It brought back the morning, it pronounced her failure. And seeing Mrs. Carstairs at last pour the tea into the porcelain cups, and thinking of the boy who had sat across the room, she was aware how very much she wanted Jamie's child. She began to feel a kind of numbness of longing that was haunted by the gentle mumble of the kettle.

"You have children?" Mrs. Carstairs inquired, as if she read Laura's thought.

"My son was killed."

"How very unfortunate. But it's all in a life. The Major and I were never blessed at all . . ." She blew her nose. "This miserable climate," she ended, as if she held it accountable for her childless state. "Will you have an English biscuit?" she asked, producing a tin.

"Thank you," Laura said. "Are you here on a holiday?"

"Holiday? Holiday? I should scarcely call it that. Though of course it isn't business. And it isn't home, so I wouldn't call it living. Now, that is a question I have never asked myself." She sounded rather gay, chuckling into her cup. "I suppose, when the Major died, I was getting away. You know how it is. Every one insists that you must get away. From what, I don't know. I was with a cousin, and she wanted France. So we crossed the Channel. She was bent upon the coast. Berck Plage was near by. But when I saw the sanatorium and all the tuberculars . . . They line them up naked on the sand, you know. It had been such a comfort to leave the torsos in Burma. Well, in a nutshell, we ended here. And now it is a habit. I come every August and stay till the weather drives me back again. I shall possibly be staying till the middle of the month."

"Will it be better in England?"

"Well, no, of course it's worse. But it's home, you see. If you're going to be miserable you might as well be home."

"I see," Laura said. "Yes, I really do."

"You are here on holiday?" Mrs. Carstairs asked, her hand on the teapot, elaborately casual.

"Yes," Laura said, "I have been touring Europe. To get away," she added, "as you put it just now."

"I see," Mrs. Carstairs replied, in her turn. Then she gave a little rhythmic laugh, musical but strangely penetrating in her guttural tone. "Isn't it odd that we should both escape to Montreuil! Such an unlikely place. Though of course it's in the guide books. I suppose that is really how you happened to find it."

"Yes," Laura smiled, "that's exactly how I found it."

There was a little silence. Outside, it was raining.

"It's at it again," said Mrs. Carstairs, looking out. "Do let me pour you another. It takes away the chill." She was tipping the pot.

"No, I mustn't," Laura said. "I must be on my way. But

thank you so much for a very pleasant hour." She gathered her purse.

Mrs. Carstairs was brushing biscuit crumbs from her chest. "Come any afternoon. When your plans permit. I was really expecting Mrs. Kermit, you know. But I never wait. We have it understood." She sipped, reflective. "Mrs. Kermit takes a drop of gin to make her nap after lunch. And sometimes I suspect that she makes it two. Well, well, we won't quibble."

Laura rose.

"Well, of course I mustn't hold you," Mrs. Carstairs said, "if you've things to do." She stood up slowly. "If you're seeing the sights, be sure to bundle up. Though what sights you have selected I'd be interested to know."

"I shall write some letters," Laura answered firmly.

"Ah, letters," said Mrs. Carstairs, looking not at all routed, looking ruddy and refreshed. "Which reminds me I must write today to Mrs. Spence. Her sister, you know. But speaking of the sights, I've had in mind for some time a little drive to Merlimont, a small resort on the coast, only fifteen miles away. Some afternoon, you know, when it isn't really pouring. If your time is taken up, of course it wouldn't do. But I only suggest it, in case you have a day . . ."

"How very kind," Laura said. "May we talk about it later?"

"Any time, any time. I only suggest it. Merlimont has nothing, really. A certain charm. But the inn here occasionally closes in upon one. You will see, if you stay . . . And then I rent a car. And Mrs. Kermit and I . . . and Mrs. Spence, when she is here . . . Arras is very nice, but it's farther away. We make it for concerts. The natives are musical. But I'm sure you know . . ."

Laura freed herself at last.

When she opened the door of her room, the thought was

waiting that in another dozen years she herself, the childless widow, would be found in small hotels—rather tiny inland places, where it was quieter of course, seeking out a stray companion for a foray to the coast, at odds with any weather, till the season drove her on.

And a rugged, dogged cheer. And an eye for the detail. And a forthright, manly air. A well-adjusted maladjustment. At least, Laura thought, may I remember what I lack. May I be spared the cheer.

SHE STAYED on at the inn the next day, not really understanding why it was she stayed. Perhaps it was because she wanted, in some unexplainable way, to reach a kind of certainty that the child could not be found. Yet, if he did not exist—if he had never been alive, or was no longer alive—she did not want to know it. Or did she want to know it? She could not be sure. But staying in her room the morning long, looking out at the rain, she began to feel already like an uneasy ghost unable to escape a scene of mortal life, where something had been left unfinished, or unfound.

Then she waited, she came to feel, as if for a sign. For a signal to leave or to search another way. Perhaps after all she should return to Paris and seek the official who possessed the word that would open for her the records at the Abbaye. Yet she shrank from the act. She wanted rather desperately to find a clue first. When she went down for lunch, she could not suppress the tremor of expectancy, the glance of hope.

There is no hurry, she thought, trying to enjoy an excellent soufflé. No hurry at all. There is nothing to return to America for. Nothing at all . . . And therefore she would wait till her heart was sure.

She looked for Mrs. Carstairs, but she did not see her. She found, to her surprise, that she would not have been too sorry to have had her for companion. During the night and the morning that followed, she had drawn a little closer to the other's way of life: the determined waiting, rather purposeless waiting, with almost the vision of the nothing at the end to have waited for.

Outside, the rain was lingering, then retreating. And finally it departed and the sky was milk haze. And the wind came sweeping through the half-quenched garden and blew it into flame beneath the lightening sky.

She felt her spirits lifting a little with the weather and picked up the bottle of beer which the waiter placed before her with each meal at the inn, though she had not ordered it, but which she had ignored till the present moment. One looked for wine in France, but hardly beer. She noticed that all the tables held a similar bottle. She read the label curiously and poured herself a little. It tasted very light; it was better than the coffee with its brimful bitter blackness that inclined to make her shudder and remember her sins.

She sipped a little more and decided it would do. When she had asked for water with her meals anywhere on the Tour, they had treated her as if they thought her either mad or ill. She had learned to do without.

Then she looked around and selected a possible Mrs. Kermit at a table in the corner. An angular woman with curled black hair and a heavy jaw and a wandering eye, who was having a second bottle of beer with her smoke. Shortly, Laura thought, she will have her drop of gin and her nap and then her tea, if she wakes in time. And her dinner and her beer and another drop of gin and her bed.

So it goes, she thought, when you are left alone . . . And so, one day, it might go for herself . . . when she was tired of answering, "What comes next?"

She looked out at the garden. And suddenly it seemed to her

43

an incredible thing that she, Laura Kendall, should be left alone for the rest of her life. I'm not made for it, she whispered inside herself. And what I'm not made for, I cannot be.

She wanted, more than anything else at the moment, to see Mrs. Carstairs walk in for lunch. But she caught Mrs. Kermit's wandering eye, and she felt with a shock that she was looking at herself.

IN THE EARLY afternoon, she tied a scarf about her head and took a walk on the wide, ancient, vine-covered walls of the city. The sharp, high wind brought tears to her eyes and would not let her think. But it gave her a kind of peace. It blew away the past, and the future as well. It left her only the struggle to hold herself against the wind.

When she reached a cone-shaped tower of the ramparts, she stopped and looked down at the bright, rich pattern of the harvest fields, the purple orange roofs of the scattered houses, the narrow streams marked by sinuous lines of vivid orange poplars rising like flames from the pale yellow willows; and far in the distance, the vapor-gray Channel, where the wind was being born. She watched the sea till she seemed to be standing on its far-off shore, and waiting, but she did not know for what. Then she drew her wind-stung eyes away and traced the winding line of the road to the Abbaye, till it disappeared.

WHEN Laura left the dining room after dinner that night, Mrs. Carstairs was sitting at her table near the window, smoking and sipping at her glass of beer.

"Will you join me, my dear?" Mrs. Carstairs said. She was wearing a flesh-colored blouse with ruffles that cradled her chins. Against the gray tweed it had a festive air.

"I watched you sitting there," Mrs. Carstairs said, "and I thought of joining you. But then I saw it would be simpler to let you join me. I like to sip what's left of my beer after meals. The waiter deserts, and I find it very awkward to go clumping across the room with my bottle in my hand to join some one else. I have done it, you know, but it pains the *maître d' hôtel*. He expects to be tipped a little extra when I do."

Laura said sincerely, "I am happy to join you."

"Shall I get you a bottle?"

"No, thank you," Laura said. "I shall just watch you."

"It's not too good," Mrs. Carstairs agreed, "but I prefer it to the coffee." She sipped reflectively. "I have always felt that if they actually tried they could grow the grapes on a sheltered slope." She put down her glass and placed her elbows on the table and her chin on her hands. The cigarette between her fingers wreathed her face in smoke. She seemed content and remote behind the drifting cloud, a little like an idol enjoying his incense.

"I would settle for water," Laura said with a laugh. She looked up suddenly without knowing why. In the door of the dining room stood Dr. Duriez. He was soberly dressed. The brown leather satchel was at his side. His eyes were on her. When he saw that she noticed, he bowed very slightly. Then the *maître d' hôtel* approached him. They spoke a few words, and the doctor left.

Mrs. Carstairs had observed them. "Do you know him?" she asked with interest. "I believe you said you did."

"I have met him," Laura said. "I had a small accident with the car, and he happened along."

"Did he treat you on the roadside? How interesting, my dear!"

"Oh, no! I wasn't hurt, but the car was in the ditch."

"How like the good doctor to be on hand! He knows the whole country. He is everywhere at once with his healing hand. And what did he do?"

Laura hesitated and laughed. "He got the car from the ditch, and followed me to see that I didn't get into it again."

"I suppose you mean the ditch, and not the car. But how like him! There are many in this inn who would give their right arm for such an adventure with the doctor Duriez."

Laura smiled at her. "I didn't actually arrange it."

"Of course you didn't. I can see it at a glance. But I love these encounters that are never arranged!"

Laura smiled once more.

"His English is very good, you may have observed. He was forced into it. The English who come here will have no one else. In fact, I'm not certain that there is someone else. And where were you going?" Mrs. Carstairs inquired.

Laura looked away. "I was on my way to the chapel at the Abbaye."

"Ah, the chapel . . . Did the doctor show you the chapel?"

"No," said Laura, "I was quite alone."

"And did you like it? The chapel, that is?"

"I'm afraid that I didn't understand it too well."

"But good heavens, what is there to understand in a chapel! One end you go in and the other end you pray to."

Laura smiled. "I suppose you are perfectly right. But the guides on the Tour seemed to think there was more."

"They must earn their tip. But one of these days we shall go together. I understand quite well what the architect was doing. He was an Austrian nobleman, who was exiled because of some nasty duel. So he ended up at the Abbaye designing the church. It is so like the French to hire him, you know. The English would never have trusted him an inch. I believe he did most of the carving himself. I suppose it was all in the nature of a penance. He had killed the other man. That explains why it looks so impossibly baroque. It was harder to do. I don't care for it myself, but I quite understand it. There are two miserable angels . . . But you couldn't miss them."

"Thank you," Laura said. "If I go again I shall call on you."

"And the doctor, did he leave you to come by yourself?"

Laura smiled. "We happened to be leaving at the very same time."

"How interesting! How interesting! Ah, the doctor!" she said smiling. "A few years ago you should have seen him. So . . . not really handsome, but a potent charm. That sturdy, Flemish charm. Rather heavy, but potent."

"Is he Flemish?" Laura asked in surprise.

"Well, largely. A touch of French, I would say. The combination is good." She narrowed her eyes, as if appraising a racehorse, and exhaled her smoke. "Of course, the name is French. For some years, he has intrigued us here at the inn. There is a mystery, you know. Some touch of tragedy. He works too hard. That is always the sign of a tragedy, you know."

"Perhaps it is only that he likes his work."

"No, no, there is something, but we can't discover it. The natives, you know, never understand English when you want to know something. But I think in this case they are not really interested. They are sunk in their farming and their pots and pans. Incredibly dull people. Industrious, yes. Reliable, yes. Musical, even. But incredibly dull, with no sense of mystery. Dr. Duriez's charm is quite wasted upon them. They seem only to care that he comes when they call."

She blew smoke vigorously through her aquiline nose and stubbed out her cigarette with decision. She looked at Laura with a speculative smile,. "There is a *chanoine* here at the church in Montreuil. The head priest, that is. An excellent man of culture and breeding. Not of the region. He comes from Gascony. I of course am not of his religious persuasion, but we have had our conversations here at the inn. '*Monsieur le cúre*,' I said once, 'this doctor of yours. I don't ask you, of course, to betray the confessional, but what is it about him? I ask out of sympathy for the man and his work.' He replied rather gaily, 'I am never favored with the doctor's confession.' I'm sure he knew more than he cared to tell. They are wily, you know. They let nothing slip."

She poured more beer and lit a cigarette. "He lives alone with his grandson, that charming child. The mother is in and out. The father is dead . . . You noticed, I'm sure, that he wears a glove. The doctor, that is."

"I didn't notice. It was quite cool enough."

"Ah, but one of them he never removes. But that, I believe, is a wartime injury. That is not what I meant when I said there was something."

She raised her napkin and wiped her mouth. She put her elbows carefully on the edge of the table. "The woman by the door to the kitchen is from Aix. She is here every year, but no one knows why. She doesn't understand or speak a word of English. But one can always convey a little if one wishes." She sipped her beer. "I have always felt he would do well in England."

"Who?" Laura asked, half scanning the room.

"The doctor, my dear. You were listening, I trust . . . Mrs. Lockhart used to come here in order to be sick. She told me, you know, in a moment of confidence—she was fond of her beer—that before she left England she would sometimes be taken, but resisted all treatment in order not to be cured when she arrived in Montreuil."

Laura listened. amused.

"Mrs. Lockhart had dreams of domestic bliss. She had lost

her husband, but then who hasn't? And the doctor . . . I understand that his wife is quite dead. Long dead."

"Nothing came of it?" Laura asked.

"Of course nothing came of it!" She smoked in silence. "Mrs. Lockhart was typical of a certain type."

Laura looked at her, unable to think of a comment.

Mrs. Carstairs removed a trace of tobacco from the tip of her tongue. "Of course, in my own case—my own illness, that is—it is out of my hands."

Laura waited, uncertain.

"My own ailment is such that I have no control. My attacks come in England or Montreuil, as they choose." She gave Laura a resigned and embattled glance.

Laura shook her head in sympathy.

Mrs. Carstairs raised the beer to her lips and drank. Then she said in a confidential, gutteral voice. "When the Major was in India, he caught a tropical disease. A parasitic thing, you understand. The name is unpronounceable . . . He gave it to me." She folded her lips, as if she summed up her marriage. "It's an odd thing," she resumed lightly, "but while the Major was on earth, it lay dormant in my system. But as soon as he departed, it rose against me with a vengeance. You might almost say it was his legacy to me."

She raised her glass and drank to it, smiling a little. "Well, one night when I was in the throes of it here in Montreuil, I rang up the desk. 'I'm dying,' I said. I really was, you understand. 'I must have a doctor.' Well, I waited, half dead, and in twenty minutes, they arrived with a bowlful of ice. A miserable bowl of ice at two o'clock in the morning! It seems they had confused me with a recent American, who was always ringing up and moaning that she was dying for ice. For her whisky, you understand. But of course you know your countrymen and their passion for ice."

"Did the doctor ever come?"

"Eventually he came. It was our first encounter . . . I owe him my life. But then there are many others of the profession to whom I owe my life." She brooded not unpleasantly into her beer. "Each attack may be fatal, it is always understood. No treatment is known. Only half-hearted measures that so far have restored me to the land of the living."

"How dreadful!" Laura said. "But I mean how fortunate that something can be done."

"Nothing can be done," said Mrs. Carstairs with alacrity. "It is only a matter of holding on, so to speak. And eventually, as with the Major . . ." She lapsed into silence.

"But I trust . . ." began Laura.

Mrs. Carstairs smiled cheerfully and gestured with her hand. "Dr. Duriez will come at any hour, he assures me. The disease has baffled science. And when you baffle them, my dear, there is nothing they won't do for you. At any hour of the night. When there is nothing they know to do, they have a secret sense of guilt. Most refreshing it is. And they still have the simple curiosity of a child. They all want to do you for the medical journals. The Major was written up in *The Lancet* four times." She looked at Laura doubtfully. "*The Lancet*," she observed, "is the leading English medical journal."

"I have heard of it," Laura said.

"But of course. Of course."

They smiled at one another. Mrs. Carstairs finished her beer and poured herself another. "I subscribe," she stated. "My copy," she added graciously, "is at your disposal."

Laura thanked her.

"May I set your mind at rest. I am not contagious."

Laura murmured a protest.

"It appears to be transmitted from beast to man, and not from man to beast. Or from man to man. So they say. So they say. But in the case of the Major and myself . . . we were close. Army life, you know, draws you very close . . ." She paused to reflect. "Sometimes it was the Major and myself against the jungle. The whole of Burma." She drank to it sadly.

The melancholy waiter was taking the order of a table near by. They listened to the short, clipped phrases of French.

"This abominable language," Mrs. Carstairs said. "Have you noticed how they spit it through their teeth? They always seem to be saying something grossly improper." She brooded for a moment, her eyes narrowed. "More than likely it's the way they square their lips for those impossible sounds. It comes out as a leer."

The waiter circled the table, gathering the menus. Then, limping, he went off with them under his arm.

Mrs. Carstairs brushed an ash from the bosom of her blouse. "That waiter," she said morosely, "has lost the heel of his shoe. It makes him sound crippled, clip-clopping back and forth between the tables. I noticed it the first day, and of course I felt sure he would replace the heel. On his day off perhaps, or when next he was paid. Not so. Not so. The weeks have passed, and still he approaches with that nasty, limping sound. I'm sure now he does it to arouse our sympathies." She leaned across to Laura. "One day at table I produced several francs. '*Garçon,*' I said. 'I want you to have the shoe repaired.' He pretended of course that he didn't understand. I explained to him with gestures. I even extended my own shoe and tapped the heel with my fork. '*Ah oui, madame. Oui. Oui.*' He took my money and went off with it, and we continued to limp. '*Garçon,*' I said finally, 'what about the shoe?' Of course, he pretended all over that he couldn't understand. I explained, with gestures. There's nothing you can't explain," she cast a baleful eye on the tables around her, "if you're prepared to sacrifice your breeding and the whole of civilization . . . He said to me, 'Madame, I had it fixed. It is the other shoe now.' '' She narrowed her eyes. "He was lying in his throat. It was the left all along."

"Did you say so?" Laura asked.

"I said: 'Then you've had your right foot on your left leg for the past three days.' He pretended, naturally, that he didn't understand."

She picked up the bottle of beer and put it down. "Let us go," she said. "This native drink is insipid enough. I prefer it to their coffee, which corrodes my liver. But I find that it puts me in a state of depression . . . Have you noticed," she inquired, "how gloomy I become? It's a steady progression. My natural state is one of boundless cheer. I love mankind. But two bottles of this and I could dig my grave . . . and the graves of the rest of these miserable people."

She stubbed out her cigarette and bleakly stared at the room. "There was a woman one season who drowned herself in her bath. They never understood it. But I knew all along it was the beer, you see." She rose quite heavily and picked up her purse and slid the strap over her arm to the elbow. "I remember that she came from the Isle of Man." She looked at Laura gloomily and smoothed her hair. "Do you know about their cats?"

"Whose cats?" Laura asked.

"On the Isle of Man." She eyed the limping waiter who approached their table. "They have no tails . . . I thought it might be of interest, that was all."

SOMEWHERE in the depths of Laura's dreaming mind, the conversation at dinner must have flowered overnight. For in the morning, early, she woke with the words of Mrs. Carstairs in her mouth: "How like the good doctor . . . He knows the whole country. He is everywhere at once with his healing hand."

She sat up in bed to brush away the sleep. And other words sprang up. "The English who come here will have no one else. In fact, I'm not certain that there is someone else."

Then it seemed to her the sign she had been waiting for. If he had practiced here for years, and in the country surrounding . . . then surely he had records of the births he had attended. He had shown a readiness to give her help.

Now that she thought of it, it seemed like a miracle that she had met him the first day, when he it was who could give her the key to her search.

She got up and went to look out at once. The rain had gone; the day itself was her friend. Beyond the ramparts, the sun was a veiled, white globe, very large as if shining through frosted windows. She stood in her nightgown, smiling and pulling her curls straight like a child. It was almost the way she used to feel when she woke, that a whole day was hers, with the heaven and the earth that belonged to the day. She called downstairs and asked for the name of a beauty salon.

After an hour, in which her hair was tamed, she walked back through the morning streets to the inn. A rapt, silver light hung over the square. The great open space was stirring with pigeons. The wind blew lightly, overwhelmingly fresh. Then it seemed to her that her coming, her searching—all was inevitable, reasonable, just.

In her room, she dressed carefully in a dark wool suit with a hat to match, to counteract the doctor's image of a wind-blown gypsy with a scarf about her head and mud on her shoes. She put on earrings, but she took them off. She pushed beneath her close-fitting hat the hair that threatened to revert from tidy waves to curls. She decided at once that in the climate of

Montreuil she could never look chic or even perfectly respectable. Studying herself gravely in the mirror of the dresser, she concluded that it only mattered that she should look responsible.

She ordered the car, and while it was coming, she found the address in the telephone book. Then she stopped at the desk and asked how to find it. But of course they knew it; any one could tell her where *le docteur* lived.

It proved to be in town and not far away; a red brick house almost flush with the street, modest but substantial, and hardly to be distinguished from the other, quite narrow brick houses beside it, with roofs sharply slanting and two narrow windows, their tops gently rounded, to one side of each door.

She rang the bell and waited. Beyond her, the pigeons were busy in the street. And the wind among the roofs was blowing up a strange sort of music, like a shrill little echo of broken harps. The sun was still heavily veiled in the sky, and its rays pure white as if they fell through snow.

Presently the door was opened. She did not quite see the woman in the dusk of the hall. "Dr. Duriez," Laura murmured. She was pointed out a door at the end of the hall.

The waiting room was small and rather crowded. There was a young woman at a desk. Laura gave her name. The woman nodded, and wrote it down on a card.

"You have been here before?" Her accent was heavy.

"No," Laura said. And suddenly it seemed to her that she had been here before. The room was somehow like the office at the Abbaye, and the woman before her like its firm, impervious inhabitant. A little chill went through her, as if it were established that she would fail here too.

"You will please to sit. I will call."

Laura turned and went to a chair by a window. She sat down

and found herself in the circle of pained and apathetic faces. Some were curious, some indifferent. She prepared to wait a long time. Indeed she wanted to wait; she was not ready with her words. Every one was silent. There was a clock in the corner with a swinging pendulum that made abrupt, rude noises and broke the quiet of the room. Beyond the woman at the desk there was a line of filing cabinets for the length of the wall. She tried not to stare at them.

She heard a distant, childish shout of laughter. And with relief, she looked out of the window into a long, enclosed yard partly paved with brick, which extended to the old brick ramparts of the city. At the far end, near the wall, was a large walnut tree, with a cloth, perhaps a canvas, spread beneath it. She thought it must have been several pieces laid together, for it surrounded the tree. And in the limbs were three children. There was another sudden shout and the branches swung wildly, while the nuts flew out and down, some striking the canvas, but most of them landing on the grass beyond. She could hear the cries of triumph and the shouting laughter. Two children, little girls, poorly dressed, rushed forward out of nowhere and gathered the nuts on the grass in their aprons, like small birds swooping on the fallen grain. And such a calling, with bird voices, to the others in the tree!

Then suddenly a woman—it looked to be the one who had answered the door—strode into their midst, carrying in her arms an assortment of rugs, which she spread around the grass at the edge of the canvas.

The children, struck silent and motionless, watched her, the two small girls still kneeling on the ground, one little boy half falling, half sitting on a branch. They were frozen all together, all the children in their game on the lawn of the Abbaye. They waited for her to leave, their life arrested. She pointed to the rugs and spoke to them in quick, angry tones and returned with head high into the rear of the house. It was clear that some contract had been made, and now revised, that they should have for their trouble the nuts that fell beyond the canvas.

Laura watched them, her breath held. Then she saw that just below the window a child was watching with her. She could just see his face. It was the doctor's grandson, who had said his lesson in her presence. He was tense and rapt.

Suddenly, with a shout, the children came to life. And the ones in the tree climbed higher still. And then began a mighty threshing of the limbs, while the children rode them wildly like legendary steeds. The kneeling girls bowed low on the ground, like tiny Moslems praying, and put their hands above the heads to protect them from the deluge, then rose with cries and began to gather the nuts that had fallen far beyond the forbidden, covered field. The children in the tree called down to them in triumph. And below her the little Jean Duriez laughed aloud in keenest pleasure. Laura's own delight was sharpened by the sound of his. They triumphed with the children. They loved them in their victory.

It was a strange, unconscious communion between this Jean Duriez and herself. Then he glanced up briefly to the window; perhaps he felt her gaze. She did not think he seemed to recognize her face. But in that brief glance, she saw it in his eyes that one of those children could have been her son's.

She looked away quickly. It was becoming like a sickness. She sat in a kind of hushed, unthinking trance, hearing the foreign names being called in the room, the clipped foreign phrases, the rude, insistent clock. She did not want to think what it was she would say, or to see the line of filing cabinets even with the wall. She was trying to call to mind the doctor's face and his grave, helpful voice when he found her by the road.

Then, in her waiting quiet, she heard her name. It was spoken so strangely that she could not be sure.

"Madame Kendall." The receptionist was looking at her.

She stood up and walked past the woman into the farther room. The door shut behind her.

Dr. Duriez was writing at his desk. He did not seem to be aware of her. She glanced swiftly around. She was in a large, paneled room that looked to be a library. Three walls were lined with books. Beside her on the hearth, a small stove was simmering.

She looked back at him. He was neatly dressed in brown tweed. In the formal handsome room, he was strangely inaccessible. Then he glanced up at her, his eyes absorbed and unfocused. It was a face that was composed, but in that unguarded moment it held a certain banked fire that made her look away.

When he saw her, he was puzzled, then surprised. He rose. He drew a pair of dark-rimmed glasses on and glanced at the file card. He took them off and bowed slightly.

"Madame Kendall," he said. For a moment, it seemed to her he searched her face with something curious, slightly hostile in his own. Then he smiled briefly.

"Madame, sit down." He indicated a leather-covered chair beside his desk. His voice was deeper than she remembered.

She sat down uneasily, striving to look at ease.

He sat, as well, behind the desk. He looked at her, his eyes gray and steady. She could not speak. There was something sturdy and heavily masculine about him, that had seemed natural to the field and the rain, but now was striking, even disconcerting in the close, somber room. She tried to find in him again the helpful, kindly air.

"It is the little accident with the beets, is it so? It has developed some trouble?" His voice encouraged her.

"Oh, no," she said. "No, not at all. There was no trouble."
There was a small, framed picture of Jean Duriez on his desk.
And a quilled pen and holder, which must have been a gift, it
was so unlike him.

He rubbed his forehead, waited, then he said: "It has not
happened again?"

She looked at him uncertainly.

"Another trouble with the car?"

She laughed, her face flushing. "No, not at all . . . Believe
me, I should not a second time call upon you . . ."

He looked amused, but detached. He turned upon her slowly
his unwavering eyes. For a fraction of a moment, he studied
her, then drew his glance deliberately away and slightly moved
his shoulders inside the loose brown coat. He had an air of
command. He was withdrawn, and yet she sensed that there
were scenes, and even words, that had unreasonable power to
wound him. She knew this, not by any logic but by the hurt
she could herself receive at unexpected times from words and
scenes and faces. It released in her a power . . .

She looked away. At times there stirred in her a kind of
triumph, and still a queer reluctance, that she could know these
things behind a stranger's face. She said at last, her voice
constrained, her gloved hands clasped upon the purse in her
lap: "I wondered if you could help me in another way."

She felt at once guilty that she was taking up his moments
that belonged to the ill and patient people in the room beyond.
She could have come another hour. She saw it clearly now. She
should have telephoned him first. But she had been so afraid of
his dismissing her lightly.

"Another way?" he said, as if he could not tell if it were
words or thought he had not understood.

She commanded herself not to look aside, but she did not

quite bring her eyes to his. "I have come to you because you speak my own language, and I am finding that is no small thing." She tried to smile. "And because you were kind to me the other day. I'm afraid you are paying the price for it now." She dropped her eyes. It was harder than she had dreamed . . . harder than the Abbaye. "And because you are a doctor . . . and perhaps would know . . ." She stopped.

Then she found that she could look at him fully. She said to him simply, "I have a reason for thinking there was a child born here, or near here, about seven years ago . . ."

He watched her, detached and respectful, his head a little tilted. And she thought there was a small amusement in the corner of his mouth.

He passed his hand across the ends of his cropped, gray hair. "There were a number of babies born in that year," he said gravely, in accent.

"Of course," she said. "Of course there were."

"But you are thinking of one . . ." he paused, searching for the word, ". . . particular baby?"

"Yes," she said. Her voice was quiet in its tenseness. "I don't ask you to remember. But I thought you would have records. I was told at the inn that you have a large practice in the area around here."

He leaned back slowly in his chair. "You have inquired at the Abbaye." He stated it; as if he knew, from the first, she had no interest in the chapel.

"I have inquired there." She waited.

He rose abruptly. "You have the name . . ."

I have the mother's first name. The child was born out of wedlock . . ." Perhaps he did not know the phrase. "Out of marriage," she amended. "At least . . . I believe this was the case . . ."

59

He looked at her oddly. "It is not so common here," he said;
a little coldly, she thought, as if his pride of place were
touched. A small impatience stirred her. She did not reply.

She watched him move toward the door. She thought he
might be going into the adjoining room, where she had seen
the filing cabinets. Perhaps he was prepared to ask the girl to
search them. He turned. "There is no name else? No other
name?"

She said, without a break in her voice, "I doubt if it would
help, but the father was my son." After a moment she added,
"I think he never came here. I think this was the home . . .
where the girl returned."

He made no move.

"Why is it . . . why you think this?" he asked finally, his
accent suddenly deeper.

"There was a letter. A note. It was signed with a French
name . . . and mailed from this place."

He had turned and was watching her. On the mantel behind
him was a gleam of copper. The tiles of the fireplace were a
bright Delft blue. She held her eyes upon them. They gave her
a kind of courage.

She said, "You see . . . I feel I'm not asking you to betray a
confidence. I can't see it in that way."

"Where is he . . . this American?" he interrupted her coldly.

She waited. "My son?"

"*Oui*, this son."

". . . He is dead."

After a moment, he returned and sat down at his desk. She
waited for him to say that he was sorry her son was dead. It
was the thing one always said to her. She braced herself to hear
it, as she always did. But it did not come. She offered at last,
"I could tell you the name that was signed to the note."

He did not look up. He took a notebook from his desk and opened it and closed it. He stood up. "It would be impossible for this day. The time is long ago. The records of that year are put away, you understand. They are stored."

She was dismissed so abruptly that she was stunned a little. She rose. "I understand . . . ," she said and paused. "Perhaps you would find time to have them checked for me." She did not like to say it, but she added, "I have come a long way . . ."

He glanced at her strangely, with what seemed to her reluctance.

"I think I did not really know until now that I came to France for this . . . But now I know it was for this. And nothing else." The words surprised her as she said them, but they seemed to bear a truth she could no longer deny.

He said nothing. Far away, she heard the children laughing in the tree.

She said, "The name was Michèle." She waited to see if he would make a note of it, but he did not move. She turned to go. "Forgive me for taking so much of your time."

She suddenly wished that she were younger, with some of the command, the courage of which the years had robbed her.

She waited all afternoon in a trance of expectancy. She kept to her room. She did not like to find herself far from the phone. He had given her small encouragement. None at all, she admitted. But still, when he became a little less busy . . . At the end of the afternoon, when his calls were all made, he would remember her plea. She was inclined to exaggerate his kindness on her trip to the Abbaye. She tried to recall that he had spoken warmly and performed several charitable, uncalled-for acts. And all the time she knew that perhaps she was beguiled by her own desire . . . that she clutched at a straw. Yet she was grateful for the straw.

After dinner, she sat in the lobby with Mrs. Carstairs and was introduced at last to Mrs. Kermit, who proved indeed to be the one whom Laura had selected.

"But I feel," Mrs. Kermit said, her eyes boldly staring, "that I already know you. Mrs. Carstairs has told me all about you over tea."

Laura smiled uncomfortably.

"Do have tea with us, my dear, when your plans permit. You know the hour and the place," Mrs. Carstairs said. "We rather looked for you yesterday."

"I believe," Laura said, "that I was walking at the time."

"How splendid! One requires it. Alone, I presume."

"Oh, yes." Laura answered. "It was on the city wall."

The two English ladies exchanged brief glances.

"Oh quite," said Mrs. Carstairs. "There's a view of the Channel." Then she turned to Mrs. Kermit. "I was telling Mrs. Kendall that we should go to Merlimont."

"Oh quite," said Mrs. Kermit, her eyes boldly wandering, circling the lobby. "It reminds one of England just a bit, you know." One saw, when one was closer, that her curled, black hair was confined in a net. And with her long, pinched nose and her thin, pursed lips, it gave her the air of being all tucked away, impervious to wind or to anything at all. Only her black, darting eyes made contact. And in them was a restless, abstract curiosity; not really quite human, Laura thought, appalled. In spite of Mrs. Carstairs' observation that Mrs. Kermit had bounced, Laura had the impression that she had died a while ago, that she was merely now entombed a little distance from the earth.

When the telephone gave a tiny bird call from the desk at the farther end, and the slight young man began to scan the lobby, Laura half rose till his eyes went past her. The English ladies watched her, alert, enthralled. She felt the little thin vibration of their glance combined.

"Excuse me," Laura said and stood up, smiling. "I think I shall read a while and go to bed."

"Some evening," said Mrs. Carstairs, "we must play a little cribbage. Mrs. Kermit has remembered to bring her board. I do think it makes it more exciting with three."

"More destructive," said Mrs. Kermit, with an enigmatic smile.

"Thank you," Laura said. "I'm sure I should enjoy it."

"When your plans permit. And remember there is always tea at four."

"I shall indeed."

"A fresh tin of biscuits came today in the post."

They seemed long ago to have arrived at their decisions, and it freed them to scrutinize the biscuits and the weather. And Laura Kendall.

When she walked up the stairs, she was no longer quite so hopeful of a call. But she sat tense and waiting for another hour before she went to bed.

IN THE MORNING, she woke up slowly, exhausted, as if her very sleep had been a further waiting. She asked for breakfast in her room, to be near the telephone. By the middle of the morning, her spirits were low.

Then perhaps it was a glimpse in her writing desk of the notice in her language of services at the Church of Saint-Saulve. Perhaps it was a memory of Mrs. Carstairs' reference to the "head-priest" of the church. What had she called him? At any rate, it came to her, as slowly she relinquished her hope of Dr. Duriez, that perhaps there was another, equally acquainted with the city and its dwellers . . . equally accessible, readier to help. And he spoke her language. That was vital, too.

She only half believed, but she got out the notice with the address of the church. She called the desk and asked a little wearily how to find it. It was close enough for walking.

She found it easily. And it looked to her much like other churches on the Tour. She did not have an eye or a heart for the differences. It was obviously quite old. And on the side, at the right, the cloister was in ruins. It must have been destroyed, she thought, a long time ago. But there were stone columns left and a few broken pieces of them lying in the courtyard where the vicarage now stood.

She was weary of these churches. She was never quite equal to their ancient interiors, which had come to oppress and even to reproach her. And she looked around slowly for another building or a small side entrance where the priest might be discovered. She found herself entering the courtyard at the side and staring at the vicarage across a ruined column covered with vines when suddenly she grew aware of shouts and laughter.

She stood very still, unable to move. It was a little like the sound of the children at the Abbaye, when they burst upon the lawn before her eyes without warning. But these voices were older, and all of them were boys'. But at once there was the deep, loud call of a man. Then a ball, she thought a football, flew so swiftly toward her that she stepped aside. And from behind the vicarage a priest in black cassock came running, pursued by a boy in his early teens. Almost at her feet the priest was tackled and brought tumbling and whooping with laughter. The boy saw her first, screamed one joyous word, and disappeared swiftly again behind the vicarage.

She found herself looking, very startled, into the eyes of the man, who lay for a moment on the ground before her. He seemed young for a priest, not over twenty-five.

64

Then he rose quickly with a panting word or two, wiping his sweating face on his shoulder as he did so. His size was impressive, when he stood before her. He looked at her, breathing heavily, with his shoulders sagging and his long, heavy arms hanging limp at his side. His cassock was wet about the shoulders and neck, and a footprint of mud, quite perfectly formed, was imprinted on the skirt just below the hip. He fumbled in the pocket and drew out a coarse square of linen, and mopped his face and ears and around his neck. His face was so red that she began to be concerned.

"Madame?" he said, breathless and bowing a little, holding the crushed linen in his hand like a flower.

She knew at once, by intuition, that he did not speak English, and her heart sank. But she said, in order to be sure or rather because she could think of nothing else: "Do you speak English . . . any English at all?"

He was watching her attentively. Then he shook his head. She saw that he had not understood one word.

"I'm sorry," she said, and would have turned away. But he smiled at her with such good will and such eagerness to serve her that she did not move. He stood before her with the skirt of his cassock slapping in the wind and his blond hair lifting. He is Flemish, she thought. He was clearly not the priest she had come to see, but she did not know how to tell him he was not.

"Madame?" he said again, and asked her something in French. His voice was deep and pleasant between his pauses for breath.

She shook her head. She hoped quite desperately that she had slipped her little phrase book into her purse. She searched for it quickly, but she had left it in her room. Anyway, she thought bitterly, there would hardly be a phrase in it for saying, "Help me find a child I know nothing about."

But he was moving away toward the door into the church.

He turned back presently and smiled at her and nodded. She saw that he invited her to follow him inside. With his eyes on her expectantly, he brushed the dust from his sleeves with violent, sweeping strokes, and the wind whipped it into a swirl about his face.

Doubtful and reluctant, she followed him. Yet when they were inside and he had closed the door behind them, he turned to her with such a depth of shy hope, and even of confidence, that she began to take heart. He was still breathing deeply, his chest beneath the cassock rising and falling.

They were in a fair-sized room smelling faintly of incense. On the bare, paneled wall was a crucifix. The other walls were lined with cabinets and shelves. She saw that she was in a place where the furnishings and linens for the altar were kept. She had glanced at several like it on her tour of cathedrals. In the center was a table, quite large, with several chairs.

He pulled out one for her and another for himself. Then he sat down before her, folding on the table his great, rough hands, the fingers heavy and blunt, the knuckles skinned, a little grimy.

He saw that she looked at them. He also looked down. His teeth were white and very even as he smiled at his hands. She was glad that he did not draw them away. They gave her a kind of courage, as if he had placed something real and plain between them that they both could understand.

Then she glanced into his clear, dark eyes, quite large and rather soft. And she saw that he waited not impatiently but with readiness. His measured, heavy breathing seemed to time the pause.

A small panic flooded her, and subsided again. "Do you understand any English at all?" she asked once more.

He listened attentively, watching her lips. Then he opened

his hands on the table, as if he offered himself for whatever she asked.

"Oh dear!" she said softly and looked away around the room, searching it desperately. She felt a little dizzy in the faintly spiced air. When her eyes reached the crucifix and lingered on it briefly, he pushed back his chair and walked to it and touched it lightly and looked at her, his face encouraging.

But she shook her head sadly. And again he sat down. After a moment, smiling, he reached into the pocket of his cassock and drew out a stubby pencil and a small, shabby notebook, which he opened to a page which was badly creased. He held it out, with the pencil.

Mechanically, she took them. She gazed at him, helpless. She knew that he invited her to make for him a picture. A picture of what? Of a search for a child?

In her wallet she had used to keep a picture of Jamie in his uniform. But she had removed it, because she found that each time she must pay for anything at all, she would find it and the loss of him would seize her again. To find him and lose him so many times a day . . . She had put him at last in the mirror of her traveling case. And there she came upon him when she was quite alone. But she wished for it now, that glossy smiling face. She could not bring herself to attempt to draw the face of her son. And the face of her grandchild she had never seen.

The eyes upon her now were sober and expectant. She began to think that he was just the age her son would be if he had lived. Her hand that held the pencil was trembling a little. She bent her head slowly and wrote her name. Laura Kendall, and looked up at him and pointed to herself. She wrote "Madame" before the name, and she turned the notebook so that he could read it. Glancing down and up, he smiled at her with encouragement.

"*Américaine*," she said. She had remembered the word.
"*Oui. Oui.*" He nodded gravely. He did not seem surprised.

The door into the courtyard was suddenly thrust open. A boy, perhaps twelve years of age, burst in, called out in excitement, and stopped abruptly. He was out of breath and dirty. The priest half rose and spoke to him, firmly but not severely. And the boy looked down, and up at her curiously, lingering for a moment, then turned and went out.

The priest sat down, passed his hand across his face, and smiled in apology.

With her eyes on the door, she was thinking of the boy: He is younger than Jamie. Just as much younger as this priest is older. . . . She looked at him deeply with it all in her eyes, willing him somehow to understand and help. And she read in his own a strange, young compassion. Very young and intense. She said to herself: When people grow older they stop wanting to help you. And she thought of the superintendent's face at the Abbaye and the face of the doctor when she had told him her need.

She pointed to the door where the boy had stood. Then she took the pencil and drew a vertical line below her name, and under it, a quick, line figure of a boy. Or a man; it was hard to tell which. But Jamie had been a little of both when he died. And under this, she drew another figure, but small, quite small. And she joined them with a line.

He looked at the drawing she had made, for some moments, and then at the door, and back again to her.

He took the pencil finally in his blunt, heavy fingers, that covered the small page, and wrote a word at the top, and turned it half around for her to see.

She read it: *Filius*.

But that is Latin, she thought. That was "son" in Latin,

when I was a girl . . . no larger than the boy who was here just now. And she looked up at him, deeply moved and surprised, and nodded to show that she had understood. But of course he knew Latin. He read his service in Latin.

There was in his face now a shy sort of pleasure, as if he made her a gift and she had received it. He leaned toward her slightly, his arms crossed on the table. In the creases of his sleeves there were traces of dust. And a place on his cuff badly needed mending. He seemed to her intensely alive . . . and present. Almost, if she touched him, the thing would be known . . .

But she shook her head at last. They did not, after all, understand one another. It was only one step, one very short word, and out of her past, there did not come another.

She would have given it up and told him goodbye, but his eager eyes held her, urging her to try. She looked down at the small page and studied it intently. She took the pencil he had laid between them and crossed out slowly the figure of her son. Her hand was trembling and the pain in her throat made it hard for her to breathe. Then swiftly she drew an arrow that began with her name and ended with the figure she had drawn at the end.

She did not glance up. But after a moment he took the pencil away. The skin of his hand was rough and firm, like a boy's, and warmer than her own. And on the page between them he wrote again. *Filius filii mei.*

Son of my son . . .

She looked at him quickly with her heart in her eyes.

And suddenly she was crying, she did not know why. To find her past, her childhood springing into this present? Perhaps she wept because a language she had always called dead had come alive in this moment. It moved her so strangely to find that dead words could rise to help her when she needed them most. It was very like a sign that she herself would come alive. It was almost like a promise that the child was alive.

Yet after all, she wept because the two of them had tried and something had been said. The heart of it, the thing that she sought had been said . . . But she did not have the courage to try any more.

He made no move. At last, she reached out and touched his hand. She stood up, drying her eyes before him. And when he saw that she would go, he tore the page from the book and gently with his thumb he signed it with the cross and handed it to her. She held it for a moment, then put it in her purse. And she thought at once: It may be that I have come to France for this. This alone. And she did not regret it.

"Madame?" He stood up. He gestured with his hand. She understood that he asked her if she would return. She shook her head. And then it was between them, like the faint smell of incense, that they had reached the end.

When she went outside, the wind was blowing with a shimmering intensity. Among the ruins of the courtyard, the vivid leaves were fluttering like birds. They swept into her face. And she felt more at peace than she had felt for many months.

THE dining room of the hotel was almost free of guests. She was late for lunch. She went in, ordered lightly, and ate very slowly. And for the first time she faced it, that her plans had run out . . . She could wait in Montreuil. It would be waiting, no more. And then, as she looked around her at the orderly tables, with their neat, crystal vases, each with a single flower, it struck her as fantastic, even slightly bizarre, that she should come to this place on such a mission of hers. She had been thinking in desperation of confiding in Mrs. Carstairs. But now she saw, in her mind's eye, the older woman's startled and incredulous look. "But my dear," she would be thinking, "such a distance to come . . ."

And after all, she would be right.

Laura finished her lunch. She sipped a little beer. Tomorrow, she would leave. In the morning, or later. It didn't matter. She did not even think of the official in Paris. The page from the notebook signed with the cross seemed the signal she had waited for to give up at last.

She left the dining room and went up the stairs. She thought of knocking at Mrs. Carstairs' door to tell her goodbye. But then she decided to wait and go to tea. It was the measure of her defeat that suddenly the English lady seemed the one friend remaining, perhaps in the world. She regretted leaving because she left this friend.

When she walked into her room, the telephone was ringing. She picked it up quickly. It was Dr. Duriez.

"I should like to make the appointment for seeing you," he said, his voice severely formal.

She replied, her heart leaping. "I could be there at any time . . ."

There was a silence before he answered, "I should like to come to the hotel, if it will be at your convenience."

"Of course," she agreed. "I can meet you in the lobby." She could not help wondering that he should wish to come to her.

"Would it be at once?" he asked.

"At once, if you wish."

When she hung up, her heart was pounding. She went into the bathroom and drank a glass of water. Then she combed her hair carefully. He must have found something, she told herself.

He must have found the girl . . . She looked at herself for a long moment in the mirror. He may have found the child . . . And she discovered that, more than anything else, she was afraid. She had not expected it, to be afraid. She had wanted this too badly, yet now she drew back. She feared that heart and mind and body would not be equal to the thing she had desired. She asked her image in the mirror if this fear and this withdrawal were a part of growing old.

She closed her eyes against the mirror and deliberately recalled the simple Latin words the priest had written for her acceptance. She wrote them down in her mind, and took them into herself. *Filius filii mei* . . . son of my son. Dead words become living.

Then she went downstairs. The lobby was empty. She picked up an English magazine and sat down to wait. But her eyes could not even see the pictures before her. There was a smell of cold ashes from the hearth beside her. Presently, she knew that he had entered and was coming toward her.

She looked up. She rose. And his face surprised her. Her own intense expectancy she was striving to conceal. She had not foreseen the look of strain in his eyes. Nor the way he stopped and took her in, a little distance away, almost as if they had not met before.

She walked toward him slowly. "Good afternoon." She was smiling.

He did not smile back. In a moment he nodded. "Good day, Madame Kendall."

"Shall we sit here?" she asked, and indicated some chairs.

He looked at them impatiently and then at the clerk behind the desk at the far end of the room. "It is better not here." He glanced around him swiftly. "There is the garden," he said. "Will you be too cold?"

His strange, intent reluctance crept into her own spirit. She could not answer at once. "Yes, of course," she said at last. "No, I won't be cold." Yet already she was trembling.

He turned without another word and led the way through the lobby and into the garden. She had not seen it before, except from the window, where it lay clipped but rustic, severe in design but flaming with color. Now when she entered, it seemed to have run riot. The great elms had showered the red brick paving with copper-and-green gold. And the beds of chrysanthemums were orange and scarlet. Even the clipped boxwoods, peppered with the elm leaves, seemed to be in bloom. It was all hot with color, closed in upon itself in a burning disorder, and stifling to the eye. Yet a cool wind was fanning it that smelled of the sea.

She buttoned the jacket of her suit to the throat.

"Will you sit?" he said. He strode ahead to a small rustic table and a group of black metal chairs.

She chose a chair and sat down. He sat down near her, but immediately he rose. He walked around the table and back to her without speaking. She was trying all the while to read his face. He seemed to be lost in his own somber thoughts.

"You have found something?" she inquired at last. The wind seemed to carry her voice quite away. He gave no sign of having heard.

The wind was dying to a whisper in the tops of the elms. "Dr. Duriez," she said gently, to recall him.

"I hear," he said, but not impatiently; rather, stating a fact that he deplored. "I am trying to think of how it is to say this to you . . . I made the words before I came, but now they are not the ones to speak." His accent was heavy. He gazed at her steadily, but he seemed to be looking instead into himself.

She watched him, her tense expectancy passing into uneasiness, then into despair. "Say them, anyway," she said.

He brushed his hand swiftly through the ends of his hair.

73

And suddenly she must say it, if it was to be said. It was for her the thing that always came to be said. In the end one must say it. "He is dead." It sounded in her mouth like a repetition.

"Who is dead?"

"The child is not alive."

He broke away from her. "*Non, non.*" He turned back. "Madame . . ." The wind was rising. It was blowing through the ends of his cropped, gray hair, and whipping the opened trench coat away from his legs. And suddenly the leaves above them broke loose from the trees. She felt them brushing gently her face and her hair.

"Madame . . . ," he said. "It is this . . ."

"He is alive, then?" she asked. She held a leaf in one hand. It was damp and cool.

He nodded; and she shuddered, but with a kind of warm returning into herself. It was the tremor of her spirit coming back into her body.

"It is this. Your grandson and my grandson . . . they are the same."

She stared at him, speechless.

"*Oui.* Yes." He turned away and back. "It is the way of it," he said.

Still, she could not speak. Then she asked with an effort: "Can you mean it is Jean?"

"Yes. Jean."

It seemed to her the burning garden had exploded in her face. "Jean Duriez . . ," she was whispering. She accepted it, strangely. She did not ask for his proof.

But he caught her low words. "Yes, Jean Duriez," he said impatiently.

"But I know him!" she cried. "I've seen him. I've talked with him." She rose abruptly. "But this is unbelievable."

He faced her with suspicion.

"But you see," she turned to him, "he was having his lesson here, and I happened to walk in." She shook her head, and suddenly she was beseeching him, incredulous. "But how could it be that I didn't know him?"

His eyes were hard. "Why should you?"

"Why should I!" She laughed a little. "Because he was the one . . ." Yet her face was bewildered.

"Unless," he went on, his voice cold, "he resembles so much this son of yours. I have not met this son."

She thought of it, wondering; as if she had not heard the bitter irony of his tone. "No, I think he does not. I think he isn't like him. But I shall have to think."

Through the clamor of the leaves, she looked at him slowly with a deep and warm surprise. "When I saw him," she said, "and was told he was your grandson . . . I believe I thought at once how much he was like you."

His eyes were narrowed. He did not reply.

"You are quite . . . quite sure of this?" she asked.

His eyes became hard. "I happened to recall that the name was Kendall."

She sat down abruptly and covered her face. But she did not feel like weeping. She was feeling only deep wonder and surprise. And a warm relief. And when she grew used to it, the relief would be joy.

But then all at once she began to tremble. The metal chair was cold against her. The wind passed through her light jacket and into her body. She tensed herself against it. She could not think what it meant, that she found the child at last. Did it mean that she could have him? Through her fingers she saw the doctor moving away down the garden. She drew her hand aside and put her head back on the metal of the chair. The wind was smelling of chrysanthemums, and now again of the sea.

And then he was returning into blowing leaves. She watched

75

him through lowered eyelids, her head against the chair. She could not move. And it came to her at once that she was at his mercy . . .

She raised herself with an effort. She said to him, when he had come near: "I keep asking myself what it means . . ."

"Means?" he said scornfully. "It is the biological fact, it is all."

"Surely," she smiled at him a little, straining to see his averted face, "it means more than that."

"Yes," he said, "but is it meaning more to you?"

She heard him in astonishment and a kind of despair. She looked at his sturdy figure built to endure, his short, graying hair, his square, perceptive face with its curious force. And she could not believe that she had traveled so far to be an enemy of his.

"Please . . . please," she said, "sit down."

He sat down reluctantly. He looked at her reluctantly. She was aware that the moist wind played havoc with her hair and blew it into untidy curls about her head. She pushed them back from her face. He watched her, expressionless. She felt in him now something that was deeply resentful.

She said in a moment, "Michèle is your daughter."

He nodded imperceptibly.

"Where is she?" Laura asked. And after a pause, "Forgive me," she said, "but don't you think I should know?"

"She is in Paris at present. She is working in Paris."

"You keep the boy for her here?"

He bowed very slightly. "As you see, madame."

After a silence, she asked gently, "Has she married?"

"No, madame," he said with irony, "she has not married."

She looked him full in the face. She had to ask it. "Were they married before he died, my son and Michèle?"

76

"Certainly not," he said. "Did you think it?"

"Not really."

"He . . . failed to appear. As one says in your language."

"But he was killed."

"So you tell me. But I believe there was a . . ." he groped for the word impatiently, ". . . a meantime. A time between."

She looked away. The resentment in his tone and face was like a blow. She was conscious that this should be an hour of fulfillment. Yet he desired to wound her.

She said to him quietly, "You are blaming my son. It is natural for you to do so. And after all . . . perhaps you are right. I have blamed him myself." She drew in her breath sharply with the swiftness of pain. "But now I have seen Jean. And it seems . . . it seems to me I don't blame him any more." She put her hand to her mouth briefly, then drew it away. "How am I to blame him for making Jean?"

He rose abruptly and stood looking down at her. "I suppose we shall be blaming your government for sending him. And my government, of course, for allowing him to come . . ." He said, with a heavy gesture, "This is what happens when you try to make 'one world.' " He stared at her, as if she had invented the concept. "There can be no 'one world.' There are many separate worlds. Everything is divided up. Like this." And he struck the air rapidly to suggest the divisions. "And when we try to force them together, it is bad. Something happens that is not unity. This happens," he said.

"What do you mean?" she said at last. "Do you mean this child? It would seem . . ."

"No!" he said. "No! That looks like unity. But . . ."

"But what?" she asked calmly. "But then I come?"

He looked at her in almost violent assent.

"Then I come . . . to divide."

"But you can not help it," he said.

"Because I am an American?"

He stared at her angrily. "No. Because you are human."

"And a woman, perhaps?"

"Perhaps."

"It is life that divides," she answered him evenly, although when she had said it, it did not seem to have a meaning.

"Yes. Yes. But you should leave it alone. You should let it stay divided."

She said finally, "I am not quite sure that I know what we are talking about."

"Yes," he said, "you know. I know."

She watched him levelly, at a loss for words.

He said, "The words are not so good. Between us, they can not say the exactness. But the thought, the idea behind the words, we have made it."

He turned and began to pace before the little table. She held herself tense but calm and waiting . . . and equal to him. She did not move; as if it were to sit here motionless, unbreaking, before him that she had traveled over Europe and finally to this place.

And then, quite oddly, as she watched his pacing figure, she became aware that deep in himself he did not want to attack her but that somehow he saw it as a kind of duty. And this sense of his duty was making him inflexible. She grew despairing and depressed. She could hope to change his wish but not his sense of his duty.

At last he stood before her. He had reached a destination. "It is this," he said and waited. "It is that in this place, in Montreuil, it is the quiet place. If something happens that is not quiet, one waits and it begins to be as if it had not happened. You understand?"

"I am not sure I do."

He tried again, as if she were a patient and he were describing quite objectively a function of the body. "This boy and the way of his birth . . . the condition . . . of his birth. One talked of it for one month, two months . . . maybe one year. But after that it grew quiet, and he has grown up with not the knowledge that his mother was not married. It has all died, this fact. And he lives as the other children live, and plays with the others. And in the next week, he will go to school with the others, and no word will be said to him. Because in this place there is quiet. The wind blows, but the minds of the people settle down to be at rest. They live without stirring up old things that happen that are best to forget."

The wind caught a handful of leaves from the elms and blew them across the table and into her lap. She looked up at him tensely. "And then I come to stir it up."

He bowed slightly, till she could see the cropped ends of his graying hair.

She gathered her forces a little blindly. "As my son came, in the beginning, to stir it up."

He bowed again.

She felt that after all she might begin to take offense, on her son's behalf. "But that was in Paris . . ."

"It ended here . . . in Montreuil."

They faced each other, hostile. She felt lost, and even frightened, in spite of herself. Her spirit had always answered a call to arms without exhilaration, but with regret and with foreboding of failure. She had been born to live at peace. She came back at him desperately. "It takes two to make a child . . . !"

He stared at her. He passed his hand across his face. "Yes," he said slowly. "You have said it." And after a moment he nodded. "It is the thing to be said." Suddenly he was smiling. They were smiling at one another, and all at once shaken with the humor and the gravity . . . The magnitude.

The wind had dropped from the trees. But the tips of the boxwoods were bristling and sighing. The chrysanthemums were rippling like a flame that surrounded them.

"It is one serious business," he said, "this making of children."

She was nodding at him, and unaccountably relieved, as if they had reached some difficult solution.

"The business is too serious for persons so young," he went on.

"I have often felt so," she agreed. "But I think we are getting old. And perhaps it is just as well that we are never consulted."

"It is right," he said soberly. "It is right." And he brushed his hand across the ends of his hair. Then he took out his pipe and knocked it on the table and filled it from the pouch. He drew on it slowly without lighting it, while he glanced at her thoughtfully from under his brows.

She began to relax, but she was shaken still. She placed her hand on the chair arm to steady herself. She was smiling at the garden. "I'm going to say something I'm not sure you will approve . . . You are not at all like Paris."

He paused in the midst of lighting his pipe. His gray eyes were narrowed. Then he began to laugh, with his head thrown back. Such a rich, deep laughter she had not heard in all of Europe. "Madame," he said, "I will tell you: You make me the great compliment . . ." He drew on his pipe and removed it. "And now I will return to you the compliment. I will say that you are not one least the American tourist."

"That is good?" she asked.

"That is very good."

"Then I thank you," she said.

"No, I thank you, madame."

He bowed very slightly, but so well, in fact, that she began to wonder if he were not after all a little like Paris.

"I shall go," he said.

"I should like you to stay. And perhaps I can order a cup of tea for us, you know. A cup of coffee," she amended.

"No," he said. "No. Too much of this . . . no."

She looked at him, uncertain, yet a little amused. "You find me exhausting?"

He said very thoughtfully, "It is not you, madame. It is your language. The subject is difficult. The language is difficult. It is hard to find in it the exactness. And when I speak with you on the subject of my grandson I must speak the meaning of my mind."

"I understand," she said. She looked away and back to him. "But I am full of admiration for the way you speak my language, and grateful that you should trouble to speak it to me at all . . ." At once and unaccountably, there were tears in her eyes.

She stood up and turned away to hide the tears. For she found she could not stop them.

But he had seen them. "Madame . . ."

She turned back and tried to smile. "I am sorry," she said. "It doesn't mean anything really . . . I've been doing this all day."

But he was standing uncertainly, his pipe in one hand, with a mingled look of impatience and compassion on his face.

She groped in the pocket of her jacket for a handkerchief and thankfully discovered one. "Surely . . . surely . . . ," her voice was stifled, "this is not unusual for you. Among your women patients."

He made a gesture with his pipe. He looked away from her

face. "I give them for it the prescription," he remarked in good humor.

"Of course," she said, and laughed tremulously. "But I think, in this case, that all you need do is get angry again . . . It is when you are being kind that I do this, you know."

He studied her gravely. He bit on his pipe and drew it away. "It is difficult to have anger for you, madame."

She acknowledged his words in silence. She said in a moment, "But you feel that you should."

"On the occasion, madame."

"On the occasion," she sighed.

"Goodbye, madame," he said. And abruptly he left her.

She waited, a little dazed, watching his retreat. But he turned and came back through the bristling hedge. He stood with his gloved hand resting on it lightly, while it trembled in the wind like a living thing.

"Madame, I shall make the arrangement that you see him."

She looked at him mutely. "See him where?" she asked faintly.

"At my house, madame. It will be better. It will disturb him the less than here, I think." He paused. "At ten o'clock in the morning?"

"At ten o'clock . . . I will be there."

When she went to her room, she saw herself in the mirror. She could have cried again.

II

SHE RANG the bell and waited, listening to the purling of the pigeons in the street, her eyes on a heap of yellow leaves against the door.

Presently the door was opened, wide enough for her to enter, as if she were expected. She stepped into the dark, rather close-smelling hall, its odor faintly of medicine. An angular woman in the dress of a servant, her head slightly lowered, was looking at her intently with curious eyes. She seemed to be the one who had advanced upon the children, spreading rugs beneath the tree.

From behind a closed door on the right, Laura thought she heard the voice of Dr. Duriez.

"I am Mrs. Kendall," she said, her tone low. She was going to add, "I have come to see Jean." But the woman moved away and led the way through a door on the left and closed it behind them. Then she turned to Laura with the guarded, slightly listening gaze of one who does not speak the language of the

83

other. She nodded her head once and disappeared through another door.

Laura glanced around her. She was standing in a comfortable but modest living room. She found it gloomy. Victorian, she thought; with its dark maroon velvet covering sofa and chairs. From the fireplace, a small stove of black enamel extended into the room. It gave off a tidy but impulsive roar, like a dreaming, restless animal asleep on the hearth. She chose a chair across from it and sat down to wait. A clock ticked from the mantel above the sound of the stove. In the corner, facing her, a monstrous plant, with a wild, abandoned look, soared out of glazed china on a three-legged stand. It held her and oppressed her as the minutes ticked away. She could not believe the doctor ever sat in this room.

By turning her head slightly she could see into the dining room, a large room beyond furnished heavily with oak. A drift of pale sunlight fell from somewhere to the rug.

Presently through the sunlight, she saw that Jean was walking toward her. She tensed to receive him and held out her hand. She could not have gone to him; she could not have risen. He walked without looking at her, straight to the stove, and extended his fingers to its round little door.

"Jean . . . ," she said quietly.

He turned and looked at her sideways. She could not tell what he was thinking.

"Jean," she said again, and after a moment, "I keep thinking how strange it is that four days ago we were sitting together, and I didn't even guess." She stopped and waited. "You were looking at the picture . . . at the grandmother in it . . ."

He had turned and was gazing at the rug between them. She was afraid he was feeling that she invaded his world. Does a child have a world? But of course—she was remembering her son—and it is terribly complete . . . more complete and more whole than it will ever be again. It is no small thing to enter it, by whatever means.

"Did you guess?" she asked finally. "Could you tell who I was?"

He glanced at her briefly and shook his head. She saw that he had been carefully, even formally, dressed for the occasion, his hair too neatly combed. It made her afraid of the woman who had opened the door for her and sent to her the boy.

She said, "It makes me think of a story I used to read to your father when he was young like you . . ." She paused for a moment, but he did not look up. "The people in the story were very good friends, who were changed by a fairy till they didn't know each other. Their faces were changed. And they became quite lonely. Till one day they found a magic word that changed them back."

He was looking at her, his blue eyes attentive. She saw all at once that they were like her own, so much like her own that she was moved and shaken. For Jamie had had the amber brown eyes of his father. She did not trust her voice after that to go on.

"Magic?" he said in a low voice. "How is this . . . it means?"

She looked at her hands, trying to think what to say. She began very gravely, her eyes lifting to his face, "I think it means this: that any moment, when you least expect it, something can change into something else. Or somebody can change . . . into somebody else."

But I am saying what is happening now. With us. She found that she was looking straight into the eyes like her own, till it seemed that she would lose herself, or find herself, in them.

He made no sign, but her feeling was intense that he understood her well, that perhaps he understood it all far better than she. She said to him slowly, "I used to know more about it. I've forgotten so much."

She thought that he nodded.

She asked, "Does your grandfather read you any stories?"

He shook his head.

"He is too busy, I think."

She was not sure that he understood. But presently he stated: "He makes many things to do."

"But not the stories?"

He looked at her silently, a little amused. "The next week I go to the school and it begins I learn to read."

"That is wonderful," she said. "Will you like to go to school?"

"I will like it," he answered.

The little stove was panting out its warmth into the room. It must have been lighted just before her arrival. He stepped away from it and presently sat down in a chair across the room from her. He did not look at her.

The servant woman, now in a very fresh apron, entered with a tray and put it on a low table close to the door. She spoke softly to Jean, and began to pour coffee into a single cup.

Jean looked at Laura. "She says I tell you. *Grandpère* said that coffee is for you."

"How thoughtful! she exclaimed. "I hope there is something for you."

He turned his head to see. "I hope it," he said simply.

It was so like Jamie that she closed her eyes and held herself tense till the threat of tears should pass.

When she opened them, the woman was holding out the cup to her and watching her curiously, with a guarded hostility remote in her gaze.

"Thank you," Laura said and took the cup from her hand.

The coffee was black and bitter with chicory. She found herself a little envious of the strawberry drink that Jean was consuming. The small, tinned biscuits did not greatly help. The room was quite warm. A branch of the giant plant shifted in the heat. She was aware of the restrained, unyielding movements of the maid.

When they were alone, Jean raised his head from his glass. "That is Marie," he told her gravely, as if it were something he decided she should know. And she felt herself admitted to the threshold of his world.

She nodded gratefully, while it came to her that this was all she must expect for the day. She was afraid to press it further, and presently she got up to take her leave.

"Goodbye, Jean," she said. She did not try to approach him. "Perhaps very soon we can go for a drive." She turned away at once, as if between them it were settled.

In the hall, she heard again the voice of the doctor. She went quickly past his door. It surprised her to discover what it was she was thinking: that he had listened for her entrance and would hear her depart.

But of course he would listen. I am the enemy, she thought. And suddenly she regretted it so deeply, being his enemy, that she paused at the entrance, wondering a little desperately if there were not some other way . . .

Jean was standing in the hall behind her. She turned and waved silently and went out of the door.

SHE SAW the doctor in the afternoon.

After a late lunch, she was coming out of the dining room and passing through the lobby when she saw him leave the inn. He was carrying his doctor's satchel. With his hand on the door, he looked back in her direction and saw her and stopped.

She hesitated, then smiled and went towards him. It seemed

to her that he waited as if he found about this meeting a touch of the inevitable. But he did not smile back. He held himself free of her, slightly formal . . . and perhaps resigned.

She responded with formality. "I wished to thank you for this morning. For arranging it for me. I am truly very grateful."

"But no, madame. It was as should be done. It was well if it pleased you."

"It did please me," she said. And after a moment, she took her courage in her hands. "Would it be all right, do you think, if tomorrow I should take him somewhere for lunch? To Arras, perhaps . . ."

He looked at her levelly, without expression or gesture. He only shifted his satchel from one hand to the other.

She reminded him, "Next week, he tells me, he will be in school . . . Tomorrow would seem to be the only day."

"Madame," he said suddenly, "I tell him today . . . I tell him at noon, at the meal, that you are leaving this place."

She studied him, uncertain. "I don't think I understand."

"I tell him you are leaving this place at once."

She heard him, her mind stunned. "But why have you done this?" she asked at last.

He looked away from her. Mrs. Carstairs was passing through the door and greeting him. He bowed to her slightly. "Good day, Madame Carstairs."

She glanced with curiosity at their rapt, intent faces.

"Madame," he turned back to Laura, "what is it more that you want?" His voice was deeply troubled; even pleading, she thought.

She stared. She could not answer, because it seemed to her that she would be content with little, and yet at the same time she hoped for so much. She had not dared to fashion for herself a limit.

"I think," he said, "that you wait and you see how much is possible. How much is possible to have."

She could only listen, speechless, to his suddenly deeper accent and his stumbling phrases.

"And I would not prevent how much is possible for you. It is not easy to refuse you. It is not easy to have anger for you."

"But why are you saying this?" She kept her voice low, for several others had wandered from the dining room and into the lobby.

He too lowered his voice. "It is not good for the boy to have before him this waiting to see how much is possible with him." He gazed at her sternly, yet at the same time entreating her. "It is like giving in his hand the power that does not belong."

She said very softly, "I don't think I understand."

He waited for a long moment. "Madame, we know it both. You will wish to take him. For how long I can not say. You can not say, yourself."

She listened. She half whispered, but the note of outrage in her voice was clear. "How can you be so sure of what I want! I have not asked myself what I want. I have only just found him."

He looked away and back. He was almost gentle. "One day you will ask it. And answer it, madame. You will suggest things to him, as you suggest this trip to me . . ."

She would not reply.

"When you are little," he said, "it is good for there to be one way to go. Not two ways, or three ways. But only one way, if the way is good. It is good to have this quiet in the mind of one way. Later, when he grows, there are many ways of which he chooses. It is not to be helped. But now should not be. Should be one way given."

The clerk suddenly spoke to him quite close at hand. "*Doc-*

teur, le téléphone." He looked at them with interest. They had not noticed his approach or heard his discreet cough.

"Pardon," Dr. Duriez said, and left her abruptly.

She turned and sat down. She watched him, her mind troubled and bewildered, while he walked to the desk and spoke into the phone. Not far from her, the woman from Aix was gazing at her steadily with profound attention.

She closed her eyes for a moment. Then she opened them, and the doctor was standing above her.

She rose at once. She answered him as if there had not been an interruption. "If I have come so far . . . and found him only to do him harm . . ." She shook her head. After all, she could not give it words. She tried again. "Or to do you harm . . ."

"*Non, non*," he said. "It is not. I am thinking of the boy."

"I am thinking of him too. Believe me I am."

He studied her for some moments. "Will you come? I have the call into the countryside. I must go. If you have nothing that is to do at this time . . ."

She looked at him uncertainly, with a small surprise. "Yes," she said finally. "And perhaps you will explain to me some things you have said."

Outside, the afternoon was luminous and pale. It was turning colder. They drove through the old gate of Montreuil and into the country. The sky was fuming with clouds. In the wind they were spewed up like foam from the sea, till they lay banked ahead, beaten and frothy.

She waited for him to speak. She was bewildered and impatient. Now and then she glanced at his face in profile, the chiseled nose and chin, the broad, high forehead. Made of stone, she thought. She told herself calmly that the logical, the clever course would be to set herself to please him. Like any other woman who wanted her way. Deliberately, she considered how best to flatter him . . .

But this is all wrong, she rebelled. Why should I act like a schoolgirl? I ask a reasonable thing . . . Besides, she thought, I am a little old for this sort of thing . . . But then if I were young enough I wouldn't have a grandchild. And there would be no need . . .

She could not help smiling.

And he said quite abruptly, into her smile, "It is well with me if you take the boy to Arras for tomorrow."

She did not speak for a while, nor did she show her surprise. "Thank you," she said at last. "I shall take good care of him." After a moment she added, "And I shall bring him back."

She was sorry as soon as she had said the last.

"Madame," he said gravely, "it is not the question between us."

"No," she said, "you are right. And I am sorry I said it."

He was silent after that. She looked at him and then away. As a child, she could not bear it if she were not forgiven. And it seemed to her that lately many long-forgotten needs and many moods of her childhood woke in her again, as if she had but put them to sleep for the short, busy years. "Forgive me," she said now. "I know that my very presence here is somehow an offense. Believe me, I know it. I know it calls up things . . . memories of things you would like to forget."

He looked at her sharply. Then he said to her quietly: "Madame, you are welcome in this place. What is done, it was done. And the act was not yours."

Then she said, "You must forgive my son too . . . Sometimes I think that what I came for was to ask you to forgive him."

He did not reply. They rode in silence with the word between them, binding them yet holding them separate and apart. As the child, Jean, was binding them and holding them apart.

But the tension between them began to relax. It could not be held against the luminous day; the sky soft-white and thick, as if a snow had covered it; the green and amber fields; beside every farmhouse, the gardens heavy with flowers that she must turn to see. The houses themselves, which rarely faced the winding road, were turned in all directions, like storybook houses. She could not think why, until she grew aware that they opened to the south. And it moved her to see them in this clouded land standing so, with faith in a hidden sun. Always, the doors, when she could see them from the road, were striped green and white. And the shutters of the windows were green and white too. The steep tile roofs were now a burnt orange and now a deep reddish brown, and looked as if a tropic sun had baked them for years. Striped and gaily topped, these houses had a childlike, even festive air. But there was always the black border at the base of every one. As if some one had died in the night, she was thinking.

But she turned from the thought to look again at the flowers. And she felt quite abruptly that the silent man beside her studied her face and was concerned to understand if she liked what she saw. She was grateful and touched.

She turned to him to tell him that she found his land charming. But she saw in his face a question, a withholding. As if he waited for her words before he would judge her. Or before he would accept her. And she could not speak. She turned again to the land and searched it for more. She was conscious that beside her was a grayness of his spirit she would try to overcome. And knowing she would try to overcome it surprised her. It was the way she had been in the old, happy days. The days when there had been in her a light to be used.

Here and there they met wagons and trucks with beets. Marc Duriez drove behind them at a prudent distance, then skilfully sped past them dodging fallen beets, while the drivers and the workers saluted him gravely. Cattle grazed, indifferent, in the pastures beside them. But once a herd of horses, quite close to the road, looked up at the car, their sleek, sturdy bodies glistening as if with rain. And a tremor ran through them, through their smooth, tense muscles, like a shadow across water, and into Laura herself. It seemed to her then as if a hand that had touched them had released her too. A flock of birds feeding on the fallen wheat suddenly rose and spiralled in the snow-white sky, and her heart rose with them. She was strangely free.

It seemed that a veil had been lifted from her eyes, and she saw the sky, the fields as fresh, vivid loveliness; but old, very old, as if they held the ancient beauty that lay in her past and beyond, far beyond, in the past of her mother and her mother's mother, till it shimmered back through her and into her son and surely into the life of his child. She felt a lightness and power, as if she herself was to place this shimmering thing in the life of his son.

She turned to Marc Duriez with the faith in her eyes. There was no way to tell him how certain she was that she came bringing goodness for the child they shared.

Briefly, he glanced from the road to her, and for a moment, he opened to her a little of his hidden grayness and let in her light. And they looked at one another in a kind of surprise, and turned away quickly and covered themselves.

He removed his right glove and took the pipe from his pocket and went through the business of filling it while he drove. It was a complex affair to get it fully launched while he held the wheel. She watched him covertly with a faint amusement.

"You must dislike it," he said grimly, "to hear what it is that I make with your language. When it does not amuse you."

"No, no," she said thinking of it. "It makes me appreciate my language the more."

"I should think it would do that," he answered her wryly.

"What I mean is that always I have taken it for granted. But then when you speak, it's like seeing inside. You light it up for me inside. It is beautiful how many little pieces there are."

He shook his head. "And I put these pieces in not the right places. I can hear it sometimes. But I tell myself it has not the importance."

"It hasn't," she said. "No importance at all. And sometimes I like your way with it best."

"Sometimes," he said, "it will not work with my way."

"Don't worry," she answered. "We shall manage somehow." She was astonished to hear how light-hearted she sounded. In a moment she asked him, "Why are all the houses bordered with black? There must be a reason."

"They are painted with tar. It keeps out the damp from the bottom of the house. Here it is very low, very damp, you understand."

"It makes them look sad."

"Sad?" he said thoughtfully. "It is against what you like?"

"It is against what I like," she said swiftly and simply.

Suddenly just ahead, there was a long, low farmhouse like the others they had passed. A little larger than most. Better kept, she thought. She noticed that his hands on the wheel tensed to meet it. And, curiously, she felt the tension pass to herself.

He stopped before the farmhouse and turned to her. "I shall be in here for a little time, but not long, I think . . . We shall leave the motor running, and the heater. But if it is cold, or if the time is long, you will come into the house."

"I shall be all right."

He closed the car door, and she watched him cross the yard, belting his trench coat against the wind. And when he laid his hand on the door of the house, she knew in herself his strange, yearning reluctance—a familiar feeling, like a deep vibration, that this house could evoke.

She turned away . . . In the years since Jamie and her husband had died, there were sometimes without warning these vivid flashes that lit up her grayness, thrusting her in spite of herself into light, when she was open to the sky and the fields, as today. Open to anyone who happened to be near.

She had almost come to dread these relentless moments when the world took her back. They left her at its mercy. She must know and feel deeply, more deeply than she wanted, but she had no choice . . . Then she would know a longing for the safe, encircling grayness of her sleeping grief.

Now she did not invoke it, but she waited for the mourning that slowly would replace the warmth of all her visions, that would deaden her awareness that Marc Duriez was moving from room to room of this house in some deeply estranged and yet familiar way . . .

But the knowledge of him held. She was wide-eyed and still, as if she were listening for a heartbeat or a breath. And something began to live that had little to do with the child of her son.

She turned off the motor and got out of the car. The wind took her breath. She looked about her. The green and white doors of the house were sharp and painful in the light, and the shadows of the shutters against the white brick were dark, but dark with depth and brilliance. She looked at them steadily; and at the weathervane above the steep-pitched roof, a dark bird in shuddering flight, clearly etched against the sky . . . written on the sky, and the sun behind the sky like a drift of fresh snow. For the first time in years she did not turn from her life but willed it for herself in all the sharpness of this scene.

The wind was like a strong, new breath in her lungs. She walked against it to the front door and knocked there gently. When no one came, she opened it and went inside.

She was struck by the warmth and a smell of spiced apples. She did not see any one. She was standing in the large, main room that must have been the kitchen and dining room, as well. A great fireplace, bordered with blue and white tiles, was sealed with cast iron, and a small black stove jutted into the room. She saw at one end a long table, well-scrubbed, very handsome and plain. The far wall was bordered with a chest with many doors. There was an old-fashioned, upright piano in an ebony finish. Small, square windows let in a modest light. The room was brown shadowed and twilit, but not gloomy. Only warm and rather secret, and secure against the wind, which flung itself against the walls like a half-mad thing.

She stood dazed by warmth, her cheeks and fingers tingling, and her ears dazed by stillness. Till above her a faint, sibilant whisper drew her glance. In the center of the dark, beamed ceiling a stuffed, feathered mallard was poised in flight among the points of a compass marked out upon the beams, his beak thrusting south. Before her eyes it trembled slightly, veering and turning back. She watched it in surprise, till she understood that it made some connection with the weathervane above.

Then from the next room, she heard the voice of Marc Duriez speaking in French. It was low and sure, and filled with a kind of solace she had not known in it before. She listened to it in wonder with her eyes on the bird. It belonged with the warmth and the stillness of the room. When it sounded, the frenzied tremor of the bird seemed to cease. But of course, she thought with pleasure, it only seems to be so.

She went a few steps forward. The room was simply, even rustically furnished. But it had a sort of richness she found it

hard to define. The little black stove was like a radiant presence. Behind it, the blue and white tiles were like a frame,
very sharp and clean and glimmering from the unseen fire, the
blue of them so deep and true a color, so separate from the
brown-shadowed, warm, twilit room that they lay in her mind
like the separate, alien words she could hear now and then.

She did not like to remain with her presence unannounced.
So she walked to the open door from which the voice was
coming.

She knocked gently.

"Come in," the doctor said.

He had spoken in English, so he knew that it was she. She
moved a little forward, till she could just see him sitting on a
great poster bed. An old woman lay beside him, the cover half
around her. One shoulder was bared, and Laura saw that he
was binding it heavily with bandage.

She said, a little hesitant, "I wanted you to know I was here,
that was all."

He spoke rapidly to the woman. Then he looked up at
Laura. "I am glad you come inside from the cold. I will be but
one minute."

And the woman smiled vaguely with pain in her eyes. They
were wandering, as if she did not see where Laura stood.

Then, in turning from the doorway, Laura suddenly saw that
both his gloves were removed. She saw the left hand, and that
only the thumb and two fingers remained.

It did not really surprise her. She told herself that it was what
she had known. But when she saw the disfigurement, she
could not move. It was not from repulsion. Rather, she was
seized with something like pity, but it was stronger than pity,
more disturbing than pity. Always, as far back as she could
remember, there had been this reaction to any sort of maiming.
It was deeper than sympathy. It was almost like becoming

herself the bearer of the crippling. It was much like love. Perhaps it was love, but she had always fought it. For when it seized her, it took away her will, and at once she was power-less; she must pour out herself. She must pour her own whole-ness into the wound. And because it was impossible, a cry rose inside her. Of rebellion? Of longing? She did not understand. But she knew it rose, soundless, till it spoke in her eyes. She felt it in them now, and she turned away.

With her back to him, she knew with sureness that he misunderstood and was thinking that she shrank from him. She went into the front room and stood before the hearth. How could he know that it drew her to him closer than her son and his daughter had drawn him in the child?

She began to walk aimlessly about the room, touching the blue and white tiles of the fireplace, running her hand lightly across the scrubbed, bleached wood of the table in the center; as if a deeper knowledge had told her she would want to remember this room. She would not think why. She would only watch herself in the midst of this pilgrimage. She watched in detachment, but the things that she touched, the tiles, the lamp, the table, became a part of herself. It seemed to her that she had shrunk from touching homely things since Jamie had died. And woven with them was the voice of Marc Duriez speaking to the woman, calming her, soothing her . . . pouring out himself.

She stood quite still and listened with a shock of warmth. It came to her that there was greater wholeness in this man than in any other she had known. His crippling was nothing. There was wholeness in his voice, speaking his own language in the service of his work.

She walked to the window. Then she heard him behind her. She turned, and he was standing before the stove and pulling on his glove. He glanced up at her slowly. "I am sorry for this," he said, and he held out his gloved hand with a trace of a smile.

She shook her head. "It wasn't what you thought. . . . Far different. Far different."

But he shrugged and smiled again, as if it did not matter. As if what was lacking had become of no importance. "At first," he said, "I miss them. But now, no more . . . If I had them again, I should find them too much." Then he added with a laugh: "It comes of the war. . . . I was making the 'one world' of which we have spoken." But he did not sound bitter.

She nodded, her eyes closed. When she opened them again, he was looking around the room. His eyes were slightly narrowed as he took it in. She watched him walk to the table and touch its surface thoughtfully, as she had touched it, his fingers caress lightly a scar in the wood. But he touched it not really as she had touched it, to remember it later. He touched it, she thought, to remember it now from an earlier time. She had a strange sureness that he had made this room . . . made it to be as he was finding it now.

He turned away abruptly and went to the round stove and shoveled in some coal from the box beside it.

"Madame Picard fell while her husband was gone with the beets to the market."

"I am so sorry."

He walked to the bedroom doorway and stood there for a moment, looking into the room. Turning back, he said, "I have given her the medicine for sleeping. She will be all right. But I do not like to leave her here alone until the husband returns."

"I understand," she said.

"She says it shall be soon that he returns."

She smiled at him. "Then we shall wait till he comes."

She moved to the long sofa covered with a flowered linen

and seated herself. "I like it here," she said, looking into his face.

He did not reply. But presently he walked to the piano by the wall. He passed his hands across the worn black surface of its case. Then he raised the lid and stood looking at the keys. And in a moment he touched one far down in the bass and held it, while it sounded like a chord with the wind, deep against the high-pitched treble of the wind. He thrust the gloved hand into the pocket of his coat. And with his bare hand, he struck a chord of his own, so faint she scarcely heard it, but it echoed inside her and beat among her memories and stifled her breath. She closed her eyes and slowly she knew the echo in him, how the hidden life within him spoke the sound and gave it back; till his memories and hers, his life and her life, were caught and held together in the single chord.

With the gloved hand imprisoned in the pocket of his coat, he turned and walked to the sofa where she waited, and sat down. And still the chord was in the room, binding them together. The chord is Jean, she was thinking. It is Jean that holds us . . . And she dared not understand that it was more than Jean.

They sat quietly for a time, listening to the thunder and the whistle of the wind. It was quite shut away, as if indeed it were caged and they were free in this place. At intervals they could hear the whispered shudder of the bird overhead, veering yet ever turning southward again; and beyond it, the even, heavy breathing from the bedroom. The deep, settled sleeping of the woman released them.

He turned and looked at her with a faint, inquiring smile, then put his head back and closed his eyes.

"Are you tired?" she asked.

"No, not tired." He said presently, with his eyes still shut,

"Am I keeping you from something? Some appointment, is it so?"

There was a smile in her voice. "But I have no one here to make appointments with, you know."

After a while he asked, "In America there are many people, is it so?"

"To make appointments with? No. Not really. Not many." She thought of it, her face serious yet smiling a little. "When I think of it . . . not really any at all." In her voice there was almost a note of surprise.

"That is good?" he asked finally. "Or that is bad?"

She waited so long that he opened his eyes on her face. "I don't know," she said gravely. "I really don't know."

He nodded and looked away. She noted how his eyes went around the room, lingering here and there on the long chest with its many doors, on a tall clock in the corner whose pendulum was still.

"This is a good room," she said. "Do you come here often?"

He looked at her and then away. After a moment he replied, "My father also was a doctor. 'When people are sick'—he said this to me—'they are like little children left alone in a house. A particular house.' I have remembered this. When I go to them, I see their houses, in order to understand . . . how it is in their sickness." He was smiling faintly. "When one is sick, the walls close in upon him, and the pictures, the clocks . . . They are very much . . . they are the world when one is sick in a room."

"I never thought of that."

She sat still, wondering at her sense of peace and the ease of the moment, as if suddenly, strangely they were deeply reconciled. And because it was so, she could say to him quietly, "I think you made this house the way it is."

He did not reply, and in a moment he straightened.

"But I think you didn't live in it for long."

He said slowly, his accent deeper, "The reason was no more, to live in it."

She turned away, afraid of her own power to sense his hurt. "It sometimes happens," she said lightly, "that we change our minds."

He leaned forward. In the silence it seemed to her that she had laid a hand on something deep within him that trembled at her touch. Yet he did not draw away.

And she thought it had been a long time since he had given his own peace into the hands of another. She drew in her breath. She was afraid to say more.

"Forgive me," she said at last, as their silence lengthened.

He turned to her. "*Non . . . non.* It is not to forgive . . ."

The wind struck the house with a needling thrust of rain.

"Is it always like this?" she asked. "The weather. Is it always so bad?"

"Bad?" He looked at her, uncertain. "But I see. But it is what we have. We have it. It is not like, of course, the south, where the sun is so much." He regarded her, smiling. "I will tell you how it is when I am in the south, where I sometimes go to see my mother in Chalosse, where the sun is so much, the whole day, you understand, so bright, so much. And the air is so still. After a week, I can not bear so much bright, so much quiet in the air. There is a dark . . . a shadow, that grows in me," and he touched his breast lightly, "to make a little shade, you understand. To make the balance. And a sound in me to break the quiet. And this is not good. I make the dark words. The dark . . . how is it? . . . the dark mood. My mother does not understand, and this is not good."

His mouth had sobered, but his eyes were still smiling, as if he found it good to tell it, even in her tongue. "But when I

return and the wind blows against my window and the day is
dark with the rain, then . . . ," he gestured finally, "then in
myself I am with peace and the light grows in myself. To make
the balance, you know . . ."

"I see," she said. "Yes, I think I see."

He laughed very quietly.

"What are you thinking?" she asked, smiling.

"I am thinking that you are not seeing much light in me
here. Eh, well! That is so. You perhaps are thinking that in the
south of France I am being in truth very dark."

She left off smiling. "I am thinking there was once more
light in you than there is today . . ." After that, she was afraid
to look into his face.

"Eh, well," he said at last. And he turned away. Then he
said, "To grow old is to lose a little light, I think."

"But is it?" she replied. She was surprised to hear the ring
of rebellion in her voice. She was finding all at once that she
too had believed it to be as he had said; but now that he had
made the words, she would not have it so.

I have betrayed myself, she thought. I have let him see that I
am one more woman who will not accept her age.

But he scarcely seemed aware of her. He put his head back
on the seat. He was staring at the ceiling with a slight, fixed
smile. When he spoke again, there was a faint, bright tension
in his voice. "On the floor which is above, there is a room
which is not finished. It was in the beginning where the grain
was being stored. The stairs are not made, but there is the little
ladder. The roof is high in the center. The walls are very low,
and the windows are but two. In the winter, the wind is very
much, very strong. It was the intention to be sealed . . . to
make a study." He smiled again and fell silent. "For myself,"
he said at last. "I have not seen it for many years." But in the
silence he seemed to be seeing it above them.

She waited. He spoke again, his voice quiet and slow, strangely free of accent. The tension had gone from it. "Before the window there is a desk, and on it there are books. One of them is about the animals of the prehistoric times. With pictures, many pictures. And one of them is a book about the saints . . . but no pictures." He was smiling still. "And beside them, against the wall, there are butterflies beneath the glass. In the frame, you understand. One of these is quite beautiful. It would surprise you how beautiful. But one wing is half gone. He could not fly when I found him. That is how it happened that, so young, I was possessing this treasure . . . Sometimes, even now, I think of him at night, how blue . . ." He broke off. "And in the desk there are locked all the things that were later . . . the things to forget."

She could not speak. The wind cried on the left. The bird shuddered overhead. "Up there," he said, with his eyes on the bird, "in this place of which I speak, there is a rod made of metal that goes from this bird to the bird on the roof. One does not see that it turns. But if one will place his hand around the rod, it is trembling so much that he seems to hold the heart of this bird in his hand."

After that, he was silent. Without an effort, without desiring it, she knew the slender rod in the room overhead, how it flashed from floor to ceiling in the damp, windy dusk. In her mind she could touch it, and it seemed to her it sprang from a deep, trembling center in the still man beside her. Startled and strangely moved, she drew herself away. Then she heard the steady breathing of the sleeping woman. And she felt that he heard it and came to rest in her sleep.

At last he went on, his tone faintly wondering, "I have not speech . . . I have not words, but it is good, this silence . . ." He scanned her face, then looked away at his own hands before him, one gloved and one bare. "The way it is, I could speak

104

the words into this silence and you would comprehend them. But the way it is, the words of my life . . . the words that tell my life, are hard to find. They are not many, but I find them not even in my own language. And in yours . . . I am not sure there are these words in yours . . ."

She was still as if she listened in the depths of her mind.

"I do not trust your language," he finished at last.

She nodded. "I have never trusted it," she said quietly. "It is the only one I have, but I have never trusted it for long at a time." She was surprised at the sudden stir of passion in her voice. "Not for the things that happen to you. Or the things you can believe in . . . Is yours more to be trusted?"

He shook his head, half smiling. "I believe it. But I can not make the promise it is so."

"I will take your word for it," she said. "It will be good to share your faith. For the things I haven't understood . . . there must be words for them so good, although I do not know them, that when I have said the words I would understand these things." She was silent for a moment, her eyes on his hands. "There must be a word in your language for death . . . a word that tells me more."

He shook his head, his eyes upon her.

She smiled at him slowly. "And there must be a word that would say how it is to be dead with your dead, and yet to feel yourself almost waking at times, when least you could expect it. There must be a word that would make you understand what this is, and why it is, and if it is a mockery . . ."

She broke off. He was watching her. He said, "There is no language like that."

"Do I ask too much of one?"

"I think you do," he answered. He was silent for a while. He seemed to be listening. "I do not ask so much. I think there is not a word to tell me why my wife left this house which I

have made for us to live . . . when Michèle is so young and the
house is prepared. With my hands I have prepared it for all the
three of us to live. . . ." He broke off, retreating from the
revelation.

They were lost inside the wind.

"In your country," he said at last, his voice composed, "I
have heard it that you are building always the house so new for
oneself. Is it so?" But he did not need her answer, for he went
on at once. "To be new is not so good. In my country, it is
necessary to have a house that is not so smooth. . . .
Smooth?" He questioned the word, half turning to her face.

She shook her head.

"It is necessary to have a house with roughness . . . that is
worn enough to catch and hold the things that have been before
in the life of the family. . . . The blue tiles." He gestured.
"The mallard, which my grandfather caught in his arms on the
lake." He smiled a little. "The table . . . you see it? He made
it with the two good hands." Marc Duriez held up briefly his
gloveless hand and let it fall. "And each one that holds the
house . . . I had it from my grandmother . . . each one coming
after makes himself to fit inside, but makes it like himself a
little. He moves the table to the end. He makes the chest for the
wall. He brings the stove to make it warmer for his wife and
child. . . ."

He was silent after that. In a dying of the wind they heard
the whisper of the bird among the beams. Then he spoke as if
in circling he found the thread they both held. "I think there is
not a word to tell what after it is like, alone with the child. . . .
Nor why I do not go to her, my wife, in Paris when I hear she is
sick . . . when in the heart I have forgiven . . . when I will
never know if she would live if I had gone, as in my work it is
given me to go to all the others and to make them live. . . .
Nor why Michèle is like her mother and I do not try to change

106

her. I think there is not a word that says I do not change her because I can not, and yet if I could do it I am afraid to make it so. Because always I have fear to change what seems to be made . . . to be fixed . . . to be natural. It is like taking in my own hand what does not belong. Do you see?"

"I think I do."

"It is a thing in my work that is sometimes bad for me to be, that I do not want to change the thing that is fixed. I must go against this. I must work to heal where it is not to be healed. I must work to make live, when it is better. . . ." He broke off and swept his hands through the ends of his hair.

She said, her voice low, "And it is why you don't fight me when I try to take Jean."

"It is natural that you want him."

She held her eyes upon his face. "Is it natural that I take him?"

He turned away. "I can not say."

"You will do nothing to prevent it?" Almost she cried out to him in a lost confusion: Fight me! Please fight me! I can not have him like this.

He answered, "I have written to Michèle. She will be here on Sunday."

She caught her breath. "Why did you?"

He gave her a strange smile. "It is for her to say. She is the mother, is it so?"

Almost, she could understand how the woman came to leave him, if he would not make her stay . . . There was a strange depth of force in him; he knew it and withheld it. It may be easier, she thought, to live with weakness than with this.

He got up and went to the doorway and looked in upon the sleeping woman, and returned to fill the stove again. The room flamed with shimmering warmth, then fell again into shadow and a fading, burnished light. The afternoon was waning. The colored tiles above the hearth were muted to the wing-blue of a butterfly darkened by time in an unfinished room. He switched on a small, shaded lamp above the mantel, and the tiles sprang forth like bits of purest sky and cloud.

He spoke across the room, with a grave abstraction. "When I am in this house, it is with me very strong, very clear . . . When I fill the stove with coal, and when I turn . . . it is with me, that she sat where you are sitting . . . When I turn from the stove, she is speaking of the man in Paris. I have known, but it is never spoken between us. It is when it is spoken, that is what I remember. And I am hearing the door of the stove being fastened, and the fire rushing to beat against it . . . and her words, his name . . . I hear it like that, all together. And the name is in the fire, and the fire in the sound of the door I close."

He was silent, his eyes holding her with a new intensity. It seemed to her that he must say it for the first and last time. And she saw it in his face that she had come to Montreuil for more than she had known; she had come to hear this recollection of a moment of pain. She had come to let him speak it and have done with it forever.

He looked around him slowly. "When I enter this house I am like the ones who are sick. The walls close in upon me, this bird, this fire. . . . They become for me the world." He stopped. He spoke again with an effort, his voice low. "I have made this room the way it is. It is just as I made it. And sometimes in the night, when I am thinking of the room overhead . . . remembering the books, and how blue is the wing . . . sometimes I ask if I have made this moment also, when I turn and hear the door as it is fastened, and her words. Did I make her words as well?" In his eyes she read a kind of supplication, abrupt, unconscious. "In some other moment

. . . long ago . . . did I make her words? Did I make it possible for her to say any others?"

In her mind, she broke away. She looked at him, wide-eyed and wary, suddenly denying him, because he threatened to overwhelm her, to compel all her compassion till she could not turn back . . . to destroy her purpose. "Why do you tell me this?"

He watched her steadily, his head lowered. She could not read his face. "I think it is a little that we are enemies, you know."

His words startled and wounded her. "What do you mean?" she asked.

He was smiling slightly. "I do not fear your pity. It is good to speak. And you will hear what I say, because in your life also . . ." He broke off. "But you will not give to me the pity."

"Because I am your enemy?"

He nodded. She was silent, wondering, withdrawing, till she seemed to be standing in a place of desolation, a place where all her losses had been gathered. And in her mind she turned and fled. Out of the knowledge of that place of desolation, she cried to him simply, "Do I have to be your enemy?"

"You believe it," he said.

"Do I? Do you?"

There was abruptly the sound of a motor through the rain. And then at the back a door opened and shut.

Marc Duriez turned and left the room. She heard his voice and the voice of another—a man's voice, high-pitched and slurred, unsteady with age. They talked for a long time, shutting her out with their alien words. She was suddenly alone.

And out of her aloneness, she too rose and went and looked in at the woman on the bed in the fading light. The hair, plaited and gray, lay still beside her like a fallen bird. Her face was a crumpled yellow leaf of the autumn. One pale, thin hand was thrust against her mouth, as if she stifled a cry. And it seemed to Laura that she looked at herself many years from now, when she lay gray and broken and stifled and old . . .

She gazed long and deeply at the woman on the bed. And deeply she knew that she must have Jean. Before this came, she must have one thing more.

The voice of Marc Duriez drew a little closer. And with its approach, she was slowly aware, as if it had lain in her mind all along, that there was some bond between this woman and him. Some thread . . . But no, it was more than a thread. They were part of a fabric invisible to her. And somehow her purpose could tear this fabric.

Her eyes went searching the small, dim room, the shadowed beams, and rested again on the sleeping woman. And out of the deep, unprotected sleep, there came to Laura a faint impression that, incredibly, this woman and herself were joined. Joined, but how? She was lost in wonder. But this could not be.

She turned away. She would not have it so. And still there lay at the bottom of her mind a vague uneasiness. As if she betrayed a kinship between them. As if she did violence to the woman asleep.

SHE WAS waiting at the front door when Marc Duriez returned. They went out into the late afternoon. The wind was blowing, but the rain had stopped. And far overhead in the pallid sky, the clouds were whipped ragged and thin as mist. But the land was haunted with a smell of the sea, and a pale, thick light that seemed to have blown from the Channel's deep.

They drove swiftly over the gray wet roads. She turned to him in the fading light. "That woman," she said, "is something to Jean."

He made no sign.

"I mean," she said, "she is something to you."

Dimly, she felt the shock of her boldness, the sense of her intrusion, but she could not refrain. It was only a part of her greater intrusion.

Still he was looking ahead at the road.

"Perhaps," her voice was low, "it was the house itself, and she was only a part of the house."

He glanced at her swiftly and back to the road. "But you seem to know. There is no need to say." She could not tell if he smiled.

"No," she said. "Not really, I don't. There was only something . . . just at the end." She sighed and laughed. "But of course there was nothing. It was in my mind . . . When the wind is from the north, I think strange things."

He looked at her then in a mingled wonder and resignation. "But yes . . . ," he began, but he did not finish. Then he said, "Madame Picard is the mother of my wife. I have given her to live in the house for which I have need no longer."

She did not reply. Hearing his words, she was suddenly afraid. Jean, she thought, is that woman's great grandson. And she felt again the invisible fabric, woven of kinship, woven of blood, and of all the fragments of all their lives.

They rode in silence. She was very tired. And a weariness seemed to possess him too. Once he turned to her. "You will speak something on the way?"

She looked at him, uncertain.

"Already I have made so much speaking." He laughed a quiet, exhausted laughter. "It is a thing you will not believe it is true, but when I speak your language for so long, the hand begins to have pain." And he held up his gloved hand and turned it a little.

"Is it so?" she asked, startled.

"I find it is so."

She was silent, thinking. "Perhaps it is not the language, you know . . . but the things we say."

She felt somehow moved that he had made her the confidence, although he was smiling and he did not seem in pain. And then she was shaken, she did not know why. And she sealed herself from him lest he turn her aside.

In Montreuil, it began to rain lightly again. When they reached the hotel it was almost night. He went with her up the walk. The rain was pattering gently on the fallen leaves.

On the porch, she turned. She canceled it all, the rich and haunted afternoon. She began, with her eyes on the dark, wet pavement, "You said at the beginning of the afternoon that one day I would ask myself what I want . . . Why should I wait? Why not ask it now?"

He made no reply.

She went on speaking, it shocked her how easily. It was as if she had thought it out carefully before, though she had not been aware of a plan until now. "If I took him with me now, I could enter him in a very fine school out of Washington, which the children of foreign people, diplomats, attend. It would not be too late. He would have many advantages. He would learn English well. He would even have French. And I would move near the school, so I could keep him at home. One year of it— one school year, nine months—would be all I should ask. It would give me time to establish a relationship with him. And after that, I think it would take little to keep it. . . . I promise it," she held her fingers out beyond the roof of the porch and sealed the pledge with rain, "I should not ask this again."

She had spoken calmly, her words matter-of-fact, as if she asked for a trifle. But he did not reply. And the air between them was heavy with something harsh like weeping. As if she held out the burden of her loneliness and asked him to carry it himself for a season. But she would not think of what she asked. She would only ask it.

He has a daughter, she told herself. He has someone else. . . .

She looked at him then, at the silence in his face. The rain was falling steadily but lightly through the dusk.

"Say no," she pled suddenly, "if it has to be no. If you say it, I accept it." Inside, she was trembling. She looked away with sorrow. "At least today I accept it."

But he shook his head. "It is not for me to say no . . . It is like taking in my own hand what does not belong."

"You have said that!" she cried softly. "And you have said it isn't good . . ." She turned to him again. "Do you leave it to Michèle?"

"I have said it also," he replied.

"But what of yourself?"

"I have said it is for Michèle."

"You are consistent," she observed. "And inflexible, too."

"Inflexible?" he asked. "I do not know this word."

She turned away to go inside. "No matter," she said. "It was not the word I meant . . . I don't think there is a word to say what I meant."

"It is the language," he reflected. "It has not the exactness." There was a glimmer of satisfaction or of grimness in his face.

"Well, anyway . . ." She waited. "I shall take him to Arras."

"I have said it," he replied.

In the glow from the lobby he stood dark and gleaming in his light, wet coat. He seemed to her ageless, neither old nor young, only this glistening, implacable form. She turned again to go. "I think that after all what I meant was 'inflexible.' "

And then she did go in, but with a wild regret, very strange and deep. In the lobby, they were sitting about the fire, waiting for dinner. They glanced up curiously; they did not speak. But she did not join them. She went up to her room. And on the stairs, as if it met her, she saw the empty space beside the fingers of one hand.

And suddenly she had a fear that she wanted Jean, because in him she would hold a part of Marc Duriez. A little of his wholeness. A little of his strength.

But that, she thought, is taking in my own hand what does not belong.

Afterward, she stood in darkness on the tiny balcony outside her room. The moon was a new sickle slicing the sky, but muted with cloud. Or was it raining on the moon? The iron rail beneath her hand was cold and wet. For a long time she watched the child moon drowning in its circle of milky sky.

FROM THE dining room at breakfast, the morning had a look of golden wine being spilled upon the earth; being poured out and wasted on the leaf-paved garden. Laura, entering the room, paused to see it from the window. She lingered for a moment. She could tell that Mrs. Carstairs, watching it from her table, heavy-lidded through her gauze of smoke, lay in wait for her.

Laura moved to the table that had become her own, with merely a nod and a smile for Mrs. Carstairs. She felt obscurely that she was held to account. She read her menu slowly, then waited, a little lost in the other's heavy presence. It was almost like a conversation between them, so laden with Mrs. Carstairs was the air of the room. She felt that the lady wished to make herself known, to reveal somehow her essence for a purpose of her own.

Mrs. Carstairs could project herself, it seemed, into the midst of the garden without stirring from her chair. She could take her slow pleasure of its prodigal, winy charm, and keep the warm hearth and its fire at her back. And thus she could be waiting, like a lizard in the sun, soaking up the best of the two worlds at once. It was a fine, firm balance she began at last to master after years of grave attention. It was, in short, the art of living quite alone: wresting from the several worlds at once their pleasures, rejecting their pains; taking the gold of outdoors autumn, with the warmth of the hearth; binding the homely glow of ruddy health to the mystery of rare disease; finding the best of England, the best of France; making through the years a little nest in Montreuil with the intimacy of home and still the charm of foreign soil. And finest, shrewdest of all: enjoying things, yet joyously finding them intolerable; easily and happily insulting all her pleasures.

Conscious of the other's mastery, Laura ordered and ate her breakfast, while Mrs. Carstairs blew her smoke against the second, brimming cup of bitter coffee, despising it with relish, her nostrils fuming, her senses keen. In that breast across the room, Laura felt a tingle of compassion for herself, so like a raw recruit to this soldierly survival-existence. The heavy-lidded eyes, while they fastened on the garden, were taking in her movements. And the mind was reflecting, "I could teach her things. . . ."

When one reaches one's prime, Laura sensed she was thinking, there becomes an obligation to instruct, to mold. One comes to feel that one can not indulge in detachment. But there it is: one desires to enjoy oneself in others. . . . It was a little like projecting oneself into the garden and remaining by the fire. With a very little effort, with the least instruction, she could find herself in Laura, yet remain herself. . . .

There was Mrs. Kendall, cut adrift at a dangerous age, on the brink of being foolish over Dr. Duriez. At least, she was seeing him, and not at his office. There had been a little public display in the lobby. Accept . . . accept, Mrs. Carstairs would

advise. Accept your life as it is. Wait for this wave of desolation to pass. Look at me. I can cope. I can wave the banner
proudly. And none were more devoted than the Major and
myself . . . Perhaps she flexed her muscles underneath the
gray tweed.

When she saw Laura leaving, she called to her manfully. It
was oddly as if she had been speaking all along. "Good
morning, Mrs. Kendall . . . It bids fair to be a tolerable day. It
has quite set me thinking of the trip to Merlimont." She
stubbed out her cigarette, smiling up at Laura, warmly, archly.
"There's a car at the garage that I always insist upon. It
behaves very well, if there isn't any mud." She spoke of it as if
it were a horse, Laura noted. "They call it 'Madame Carstairs'
little Dauphine,' although I understand they have only one
Dauphine."

Laura stood in the current of warmth from the fire. "How
pleasant it sounds!" She hesitated, then decided to be perfectly
frank. "As a matter-of-fact, I have planned a little trip to Arras
for today . . . Perhaps you will be going to Merlimont again."

Mrs. Carstairs regarded her sharply, with interest. "Arras,"
she repeated. "Of course, of course." Then underneath her
tweed, she flexed her muscles again. "Alone, I suppose?"

Laura said easily, "No, I'm going with someone. Otherwise, of course, I could put it off."

"Someone from the inn?"

"Oh, no one from the inn."

There was a brief, strained pause. Mrs. Carstairs began,
"Do sit down for a moment. If you have the time."

"I have a little laundry that is crying to be done . . ."
However, Laura sat on the edge of the chair. "I promised
myself that before I left . . . I put off the things I don't like to
do."

"And you do the things that you like to do." Mrs. Carstairs

had spoken with a deep implication. With fine deliberation, she lit a cigarette. "Coffee?" she inquired, her tone rather hoarse.

"No, thank you. One cup, half milk, is quite all I can manage."

Mrs. Carstairs turned around and opened her purse, which was hanging by its strap from the back of her chair. She groped in it blindly, her eyes half closed. At length, her hand emerged with a long yellow holder, into which she proceeded to insert her cigarette. In spite of herself, Laura felt impressed. She sensed that the holder was reserved for occasions.

Mrs. Carstairs held herself abruptly erect. "Army life," she observed, "has taught me many things." She seemed to suggest that she had drilled with the troops. But she did not go on with it. She placed the holder in her teeth. Then she made a little face, and removed it and wiped the mouthpiece with her napkin, delicately, thoughtfully. "The doctor, I suppose, has a patient in Arras."

Laura heard her, astonished; that is, she tried to be astonished. She began to examine the point of the remark. Finally, she said, her voice strained, "I'm not going with the doctor. If that's what you mean."

"Oh?" Mrs. Carstairs said, lifting her brows. She did not commit herself entirely to belief. Her fire had gone out. She lit it again and deeply inhaled, her face entranced, till she seemed like a sybil engaged with her oracle. Then she suddenly emerged and laughed with a gracious, little bounding chuckle. "I naturally assumed, since it was no one from the inn . . . and thinking, of course, that you had not had time to make other friends . . . But we are always inclined to underestimate Americans. I remember there was one year a lady from Boston . . . though I believe it was actually a suburb of Boston . . . which makes it more credible . . ." She did not go on.

117

Laura said, her fingers gripping the rim of her purse, "Since you seem to take an interest . . . I'm sure it's more than kind . . ." But she gave it up. She was too poor with irony. And looking at the older woman's weathered face with its heather-pink flush, its arrangement of veins, she could not quite reject her. She felt herself close to the brink of something final. And only youth could indulge itself with making an enemy. Only youth could afford to find itself outraged. She tried to speak calmly, though her tone was hardly kind. "It's the doctor's grandson I'm taking to Arras." Then she looked at the fire. "Today is my birthday, as a matter of fact."

When she turned back, Mrs. Carstairs was gazing at her, incredibly shocked.

Laura suppressed a small, hysterical tremor. "What is it?" she said. She could not resist asking. She wanted badly to laugh.

Mrs. Carstairs put down her cigarette. Her hand was trembling. "Well now, of course . . ."

Laura looked at her expectantly.

Mrs. Carstairs cleared her throat. "It's just that I shouldn't think of using the child."

Laura smiled. Her throat was tight. "It doesn't seem fair play."

"Well, not really sporting," Mrs. Carstairs agreed.

"I suppose Mrs. Lockhart would not have stooped so low."

There was a palling silence. And suddenly, unbelievably, they burst into laughter . . .

Mrs. Carstairs was wiping her streaming eyes. "Mrs. Lockhart never thought of it. She was really quite stupid." She blew her nose. "To think," she added weakly, "that I introduced the two of you. You and young Duriez."

Laura said lightly, "I am indeed having a birthday today."

"I never doubted it for a moment, my dear."

"It's perfectly true. I'm being forty-five."

"Felicitations!" Mrs. Carstairs said. "Or rather, condolences. Whatever you wish." She picked up her cigarette. The fire was out, and she abandoned the holder, which she tossed unceremoniously into her purse. "To be perfectly frank," she said of the holder, "it tastes very strongly of moldy bread. I save the crumbs, you know, for the birds at my window. I make a practice of dropping them into my purse . . . The crumbs, that is. Oh dear, not the birds . . ." She was off again in a spasm of gutteral mirth.

Laura watched her, beguiled. "Do you think you shall go to Merlimont today?"

"I really can't say. It will all depend . . ."

"Because if you aren't, I shall ask for the little Dauphine again."

Mrs. Carstairs straightened. There was a dangerous pause. "I don't consider that I own the car." All the same, she was close to being affronted. Then soberly she recalled that she was no longer with the Army; that she had lost her priorities when she lost the Major. She decided, after all, to be generous with the car. "Take it, my dear. Take it to Arras. . . ." Then she inserted a bit of irresistible malice: "The petrol gauge will lie to you. I wouldn't trust it."

"Thank you," Laura said. "I shall be on my guard." She rose and smiled. "Advise me," she said, "about a place to lunch."

Graciously, Mrs. Carstairs allowed herself to be won. "Oh, the Hôtel du Monde, by all means, by all means! It's on the Croix-Rouge, a tiny little passage off the rue Saint-Aubert." She traced it on the cloth with the edge of her fork. "Here . . . precisely here. Oh, but stop and ask. The little Duriez will interpret. Such an excellent lad!" And she tossed aside the fork in her hearty, English admiration of the well-reared child.

LAURA picked Jean up at ten in the little Dauphine. It had begun to rain. He was brushed and very clean and very, very formal. He allowed her to hold an umbrella over his head. And she sensed that he was burdened with some freshly spoken word about the care of his suit.

On the way, she explained to him about her birthday. He did not know the word. When he understood, he looked at her, wondering, relaxing. She felt his movement toward her at some deeper level: she had not always existed; she had been born like himself.

"What do you call it?" she asked him. "What is 'birthday' in French?"

"Madame Spence, she have told that it is *anniversaire*."

"*Anniversaire*." She repeated it awkwardly. "It sounds more important. I shall call it that."

Then she wanted to ask him the day of his own birth, but she did not have the courage. Not now, not yet, while she stood in the past. For all at once she would seem to be asking about Jamie, prying into the month, almost the day he made love to a girl he had not wanted her to know of . . . or he would have written.

But she said, "Do you ever have a party on your *anniversaire*?"

He looked up at her. "A party?"

"Like this today, you know. A special dinner. And a special dessert."

"*Ma fête*? But I am called for *Saint Jean*. It is on his day *ma fête*."

"But is it like this with everyone?"

"Oui, with all . . . I think."

She shook her head. She said simply, "I think I like my way best."

He answered her soberly. "I would like it being two." He held up his fingers.

"Both of them a *fête*?"

He nodded.

She laughed aloud. And she found that she loved him, as if she had known him from the unknown, wonderful day he was born. It made her grow afraid; it left her speechless before him.

In the Hôtel du Monde, they sat in the pleasant, rustic dining room, and beyond them through the glass, at the mercy of the rain, lay the sodden little garden for summer dining.

He laid his chin upon his opened menu and gazed at all the room, at the waiters and the guests. He seemed to be at home, as if he had been taken here before perhaps. But he had seemed almost as much at ease in Mrs. Carstairs' room; she hoped it was his nature. He might even feel at home in America, she dreamed.

She glanced about her too. It was really quite charming. More spacious than the inn, and with a lively air, as if the guests were younger. The long, lilting draperies were molten leaf and flower that splashed upon the floor. And all around the room, beyond the little garden, the city seemed to press and to brood above this place. And the rain closed them in. The gay little company was sitting warm and lighted, an oasis of the city in the heart of rain. There was a tremor of climax. There was a feel of spring. But perhaps it was because she was here with Jean, and she needed to have a sense that all was just beginning . . .

He was gazing now at her. "How many years have you?"

She looked into his small, sturdy face like his grandfather's;

into his blue, observant eyes, so like her own that she could lose herself, or find herself, in them. "Forty-five," she answered.

He did not reply.

"It is many years," she added, smiling at him a little.

"Yes," he said; and after a moment, carefully, "It is many years, but you not speak . . . do not speak French."

She nodded gravely. "I am ashamed to be so old and yet to speak only my own language." She read agreement in his eyes. "In America, we are not taught to speak other languages. Not as you are taught. I am glad you are learning mine. . . Shall you learn any others?"

His bright eyes were on her lips. "I shall wait. In some years I shall speak them."

When the waiter arrived, she picked up her menu and smiled at Jean. "Order anything," she said. "Anything you like. And for me, the same."

Jean looked down at his menu and up at the waiter. But of course, she thought, he is only seven and he does not read his French. Somehow, ridiculously, it made her feel a little better. She folded her menu.

"I want you to have whatever you like best."

He looked at her; half frightened, she thought. But she smiled with encouragement, in league with him deeply. Waiters had always frightened her a little. Even in America, when they stood with pencil poised at her side, she sometimes lost conviction that she wanted what she ordered.

"Pretend," she said, ignoring the looming figure beside them, "that it is your *anniversaire*, and not mine. Or your *fête*. Then think what you would like."

"I have not hunger," he said, his troubled eyes on her face.

She nodded slowly. "I have not, either," she answered, and it was suddenly quite true. She glanced up at the melancholy,

122

alien presence. He did not even look French. But she could see that he spoke English, or understood it well enough. "Bring us something," she said. "Whatever you think the boy would like to eat."

"*Oui*, madame." He bowed slightly, and disappeared at once as if she had offended him.

She tried a little desperately to remember how she had conversed with Jamie when he was little, what things they had talked of. But in an alien land it did not seem the same . . .

"How pretty this room is!" she exclaimed. "And these flowers on the table . . ." She touched one lightly and felt it shudder through its petals. Or was it her own fingers? For there was in herself again, as in the garden of the Abbaye, a little shiver, like a vibrating, indrawn breath. It seemed to her that this, this present, might be the most that she would have of Jean, and she knew she was afraid of afterwards remembering that she had let it slip away.

The weight of it, her tenseness, oppressed him, she could see. And her gaiety, in spite of it, seemed to make him ill at ease.

"Jean," she said at last, looking into his face, "I used to have a boy to talk to, but it has been so long ago I have forgotten how to do it." She did not try to smile. "But I like to be with you . . . ," her voice faltered, "very much."

He nodded slightly.

"You can tell that?" she asked. "You can see that I do?"

"*Oui*," he answered, his eyes wide and strangely bright on her face.

"Then it is enough," she said, wondering. "We won't need to sound like friends . . ."

After that, they were silent. In a room far away, there was a tinkling of glasses. Through the glass doors to the terrace she could see the rain misting on the leaves and the flowers, and the sunlight paling through it, so that suddenly it looked as if the sun itself were misting. This is lovely, she was thinking. I shall remember it like this. The tinkling of the glasses was like a fine mist of sound. And the presence of the child was like a mist in her heart, warm and familiar. For the first time, she knew finally that she wanted to have him. She had thought so before. But her thinking was as nothing to her deep conviction now. All at once, she wanted him so much that she was frightened and told herself that nothing, nothing in this life is possessed . . . that everything is given for a time. For a time.

The waiter was upon them, around them, between them, mysterious, expansive . . . not, after all, offended. Far from it; he bore gifts for them. Each dish he uncovered was an offering, a surprise. He refrained from "*Voilà!*," but Laura almost said it for him, so much it asked to be said. And it was one of her French words, though she did not really trust it.

"What is it?" she asked him. "It smells so very good."

He smiled with his secret. "Does the little one know? It is the eel with green sauce. Very special, madame."

Jean gazed at her gravely. "Marie makes it," he said, "when *Monsieur le curé* comes."

"When he comes to dinner, does she?"

"She makes it on that time. And for *Maman*, when she comes."

"For your mother?" she asked.

He nodded.

"Is it often that she comes?"

He thought of this for a moment. "It is . . . *quelquefois*," he said.

"When is that?" she asked him.

He shook his head above the plates. He could not think of the word. He said slowly, "It is almost when ones does not remember it came before."

"I see," she said.

They fell to eating, while the waiter brooded over them from a distance, detached and yet alert. He pretended not to see them, but not a movement escaped him, not the flicker of an eyelid.

"Is your mother . . . is she pretty?"

He chewed and looked puzzled.

"Is her face very pretty?"

"Face?" he said.

"Yes. Face." She smiled and touched her own, and then his, with the back of her finger.

He laughed and looked to see if the waiter had observed them. "I not remember," he said.

"This is so good," she told him. "I'm glad we left it to the *garçon*. What did he say it was? I couldn't understand what it was with green sauce."

"I have not the words for what is eaten."

"Oh, but that is a shame. When you come to visit me in America, you will get hungry, you know."

She watched him closely when she said it, but he gave no sign. After a moment he asked, without glancing from his plate, "When is it I shall go?"

She kept her voice casual. "Oh, very soon, I hope." And she held her breath.

He seemed to have accepted it. He went on eating. He looked up, his eyes bright. "What this is . . . it is this." And he held out his arm and moved it slowly through the air in an undulating gesture.

"But it can not be an arm we are eating, Jean."

He laughed aloud. "*Non, non.*" He traced a wiggling line on the cloth with his finger.

"But surely not a snake . . ."

"I not know the word for which we eat."

125

"Oh dear," she said, "could it be an eel?"

"I not know the word."

"I think it is," she said slowly. "I think he said it was eel."
She put down her fork, then picked it up again. "No matter,"
she announced. "It is very, very good . . . Do you like it?" she
asked.

"*Oui*, I like it," he said.

"Then I shall like it too." She sounded brave and determined.

Presently she asked, "What will you do tomorrow? You will
go to church, I'm sure."

He nodded.

"With your grandfather?"

"*Oui*. And *Maman*."

"Oh?" She waited, her heart still. "She will come in time
for church?"

"*Oui*, she will come this night."

After a moment she asked, "Does your mother speak English?"

He shook his head.

"But she speaks a very little?"

"*Non*, not English," he said. "She speaks French."

"Of course."

"And one little German."

"But I was thinking that perhaps she spoke a little English."
She was suddenly aware that she was almost pleading.

He laughed abruptly. "She know two words."

"What are they?" she asked.

" 'Good day' and 'goodbye.' "

"Oh dear," she said. "That is not very much."

He seemed deeply amused. "It is all the words she say to me
when I speak English to her. She say it is one bad language."

"Does she? Does she say that?"

"*Oui*, she not like it." He looked at her, thinking. "She say she one time know more words. But not now no longer."

"And have you tried to teach her?"

"She wish that she not learn."

She touched the beer that had been placed before her to her lips and put it down. "And does she care if you learn it?"

He shook his head decidedly. "*Non*, she say . . ." He stopped, puzzled. "I can not say it in English, what is." He thought of it for a moment, his eyes narrowed. He laughed. "But she not care if I learn it. She not care what I do."

"But of course she does. She cares a great deal what you do."

He said firmly, his eyes merry. "If I not . . ." He stopped and looked at her. He laughed and struck his palms together, his eyes on her own.

"Make noise?" she asked.

He looked doubtful.

"Make a big sound?"

He laughed again, pleased. "If I not do this, she not care." He was somehow released.

It surprised and amused her, to see how he shifted from a grown-up sort of child to one who seemed younger, when his English words failed him. She was laughing with him. "You haven't made a big sound today. You have been very quiet. Silent."

"*Oui*," he agreed.

"You have been thinking of school next Monday and how silent you must be."

He thought of it soberly. "*Non*. It is not."

"No," she said, smiling. "For I have been silent, too."

And suddenly she was looking straight into his eyes like her own, and remembering the words of Marc Duriez: "I have not speech . . . I have not words, but it is good, this silence." And it took away her breath to be reminded again that this child before her was so much like Marc Duriez and herself. So little like Jamie.

She caught a glimpse now of a kind of still delight in the depths of his eyes that were made of her own. It was there without warning, a point of concentrated blueness. It was as if he gathered himself closely, and waited in readiness to receive a special gift.

"What is it?" she asked.

He shook his head. He turned and looked at the waiter, who started and relaxed, and then around the room, and back again to her, and still it was the same. The eyes, she had given him; but not this delight.

"Tell me," she said. For she wanted to share it.

But he gazed at her, surprised. And she understood at once that it could not be told. His gaze wandered again, with the deep, sure rapture that seemed to spring from everything he chanced to behold. Yet it could not be chance that these things were at hand.

She watched him, her breath held. Mirrored in his eyes was a moment she half remembered, but it was so long ago that the search for it was painful . . . He seemed to take it into some center of his vision: The misting rain beyond the glass shaded gray against the trunk of the lone terrace elm, tinted lemon in the sun. The waiter lounging by the wall like a bit of steel spring uncoiled for the moment. The flowers on the table that trembled with the brilliance of their deep sun-gold. All of it belonged to him deeply and surely. Without question, he took it in, this stillness of delight.

But this is how it is to be a child, she remembered. You are always being given the heart of things forever. You are always

128

at the mercy of moments like this. Before you learn that everything is given for a time . . . and will be taken away.

But I remember it, she thought with a deep, uneasy wonder, her eyes on his face. Perhaps if it was in me, I have given it to him . . .

And then she was more afraid of losing him now. As if, in losing him, she would lose herself.

The waiter had slipped upon them and removed their plates. Unexpectedly, with an athletic ease, he produced for them a towering dessert. It was a golden, sculptured thing, yet intricate and shimmering with a subtle sort of life. It made her think of the carvings in the church at the Abbaye. But it was more like the angels that had hovered overhead.

She was in awe of it a little. She smiled up at him. "What is it?" she exclaimed. But she did not understand him when he told her, of course.

He circled them, gracious. He was as pleased and shy as they. "It is chosen for madame."

"But how nice! How very nice! Isn't it splendid, Jean! He was listening when I said it was my *anniversaire*."

Jean beheld it, his face shining but not really surprised, as if it only climaxed his own particular delight. And both of them were smiling at her, the boy and the waiter, who somehow, in the depths of his somber smile, she could see, was a shy and lonely man, who had outlived his own occasions but who now and then enjoyed a customer's as if they were his own.

She raised the spoon and put it down. "It is too beautiful to eat." And the three of them were laughing softly, bound together, deeply held; and she was flooded with warmth. For she had never been able to maintain the rigid barriers: between the young and the old, between the server and the served. It was because she rarely felt them, though often she pretended.

129

Then the waiter, with an infinite, deliberate grace, lifted the spoon and gently cut into the dish and laid it open for her. It gave an audible sigh. His hand was trembling when he served it.

She ate it slowly, with a mist in her eyes. She was thinking that if it had really tasted as good as it looked, she could not have borne it. She would have cried a little.

And all at once she was at home here in France with the child. She looked in deep surprise at the waiter's retreating back, and then at Jean who was absorbed in the splendid ruin of dessert. I can feel things again, how good they can be . . . Beyond her, the rain flashed its silver on the terrace. And for one poignant moment, she allowed herself to dream that she would never leave . . .

"When is your *anniversaire*?" she asked, shaken with the dream.

He looked at her and shook his head.

"But everyone was born on a certain day."

"I not know the words."

"But you can count in English."

"I not know the . . . all."

"The months . . . I see. But was it hot or was it cold on your *anniversaire*?"

"It was raining," he said.

"I believe it," she answered. And suddenly they were, both of them, laughing like sillies. And beyond them the somber waiter sprang alert with a spirited glance, in league with them, amused.

"I show to you," said Jean, and he drew from the pocket of his trousers a small object, which he held for her to see in the palm of his hand.

"What is it?" she asked, leaning over it, merry. She was somehow enchanted that his hand was grubby.

130

"It was given for *ma fête*."

"But what is it?" she asked. "Is it some sort of stone?"

He watched her, delighted. "*Un oeil-de-chat*," he said at last.

"Jean! Say it in English."

He shook his head. "I can not," he answered. With his free hand he made a round hole for one eye, and gazed at her through it, his other eye closed.

"Oh, Jean!" she cried, laughing. "You could tell me, I know." It always seemed to please him when he could not find the English words. That is not like his grandfather, she could not help thinking.

Then the waiter was upon them with the bill in the tray, and was staring discreetly into the open palm. "*Splendide!*" he said with dignity and a ring of enthusiasm, perhaps of congratulation. "*Splendide!*" he added. "*C'est un oeil-de-chat.*"

She stared with the waiter, trying to see it with his knowledge and approval. But she burst into laughter, she could not tell why. It was wonderful, even preferable, not to know what it was.

"Who gave it to you?" she asked.

"Marie gave it," he answered. "The brother of Marie found it in one far country. He found it for me. He is one good friend."

She sobered a little. She reached into her purse and took out some bills and put them on the plate the waiter had brought. "What do you use it for?" she asked almost absently, a chill on her heart.

When she looked again, Jean had taken the object and placed it to cover up one blue eye.

"Oh dear," she said, "now it looks like an eye."

He laughed quite joyously. "*Mais oui*," he cried, "it is the eye of the cat! *Voici*, it is seeing you out of the stone."

131

"Of course," she said.

Then it seemed to her the tiny stone held in its heart a faded blue bit of a butterfly's wing. Like an echo of all that was innocent delight. Like an echo of the happiness of Marc Duriez.

She waited for a moment. "Shall you miss Marie if you come to America?"

He nodded at once. "She will come with us, is it so?"

She looked away. Outside, it was raining with a delicate monotony. "I don't know," she said slowly. "We can ask her, though."

On the drive home she found they had lost the communion. They scarcely spoke. But in the small, silent form of Jean, increasingly for her Marc Duriez was present. I imagine it, she thought. But still there persisted a fine, faint aura of the grandfather's presence. Perhaps, more exactly, it was the child that had been. The child of the blue-winged butterfly, when first it was captured and delighted in. And she could not be certain for which of these children her yearning was deeper.

The rain had stopped before they reached Montreuil. She walked with Jean to the door of his house. When she rang the bell, she asked on impulse, "Is your grandfather in his office on Saturday afternoons?"

He looked up, thinking. "I not know. I not remember."

And then the door was opened, and Marie was in the shadows.

"Good afternoon," said Laura. She hesitated. "May we ask Marie if he is?"

He looked at her, uncertain.

"Ask her if your grandfather is in his office now."

He nodded and spoke quickly. Marie shook her head, her eyes from the dark hall hostile and staring, yet curiously

132

withdrawn; as if she were a painting, Laura thought with surprise. One of countless, painted faces from countless walls on her tour, that had seemed from out the shadows to pass a mindless judgment.

She turned away. "Goodbye, Jean . . . Goodbye, my dear." She did not look back. From the face in the shadows, Marc Duriez had seemed to speak. The eyes pronounced a judgment he had stifled in his own.

If I had found him in his office, what should I have said to him, standing by his desk in the late afternoon? And then she knew clearly that she had nothing to say; that she had wanted but to see him and to hear his voice.

She got into the car and drove swiftly away. Before her, the iridescent pigeons lingered on the pavement till it was almost too late, then splashed suddenly upward, as if she had tossed a stone into the midst of shallow waters. In the distance she caught a glimpse of the young *abbé* on his bicycle, swaying on the cobblestones, rounding a corner. Below a leather jacket the skirt of his cassock swelled abruptly in the wind, like the wings of the pigeons starting up from her path.

And seeing him, it seemed to her, with a tightness in her throat, that when you are young and have your life before you, you are content to wait for people to become for you what, in time, they will become. Wait and see, you can say. But when you are poised on the brink of middle life, and time is running out, you can no longer wait. You must discover it now. If this is enemy, you must know it. If this is friend, you must know. You must ring the doorbell and ask, "Is the doctor in his office?" You must turn away with sorrow, because you must wait.

Nothing can ripen slowly. It must happen now. As she stepped from the car, she caught a glimpse of herself—in her mind's startled eye—standing on tiptoe, poised on the brink, and holding out her hands for the whole of it now.

133

And when, beyond the shelter of the garage, she felt again the wind, it was as if it struck her with a great force of longing, of yearning. But for what? She could not say. But her body quivered with the singing, salty keenness of the wind, as if it were the sea itself, concentrated, distilled, that dashed itself against her and would not be held . . . that probed her and questioned and drowned her reply.

And yet deep inside her there remained the still delight that had matched Jean's own. Like a tiny ocean plant firmly rooted in the rock, that could not be loosened or swept away.

Later, after supper, she called the office of Marc Duriez. He answered at once. He was working late.

She held her voice steady. "This is Laura Kendall . . . I understand from Jean that his mother is arriving. If she has come, will you ask if she will dine with me tomorrow. At one o'clock at the inn."

There was a momentary silence. "Madame, you understand . . . my daughter speaks no English."

"I understand. I shall be grateful if you will somehow arrange for me . . . this meeting."

"One moment, madame." He put down the phone. And then she waited for a while. She thought she heard the muffled roaring of the black enameled stove on his hearth. She saw the books on his walls. At last she held in her mind the photograph of Jean she had seen on his desk.

She heard his voice. "It is arranged. She comes."

His tone was so formal. She wanted suddenly to ask him what his daughter was like. She wanted rather badly that he should not hang up.

She found herself saying, "I'm a little bit afraid." She heard the words; and she would have recalled them, but of course it was too late.

He did not answer.

134

"Are you there?" she asked.

"Yes, madame." It was the voice that had spoken of a room left unfinished . . . of his life unfinished.

"I seem to be always asking you to help me . . . Good night."

"Good night, madame."

But he did not hang up. She listened to his silence. And she hung up quietly. There were tears in her eyes.

She sat without stirring, knowing with deep certainty that he too waited . . . so close that she might have reached out and touched him. She laid her fingers on the cradle of the phone. She was filled with swift longing for the touch of his hand. Then it seemed to her that all her life had been lived for this moment. Not for finding her grandchild . . . but this strange communion.

ALL MORNING long the bells for church had been ringing.

Laura waited in the lobby for Michèle to arrive. It was after one o'clock. The clock above the desk had struck and grown still.

She isn't coming, Laura thought. And she did not know whether to despair or rejoice. She could hear the busy little murmur of the diners. There were more of them on Sunday. Whole families of the townspeople had appeared when the ringing of the bells had ceased. Now the lobby was empty.

Then she was seeing Michèle as she walked through the door. And the murmur of the diners became for her one voice . . . one continuous word, which she tried to understand.

She gazed at her, a small figure of a girl with very dark hair, entering slowly, her dark eyes swiftly circling the lobby. Uncertain she was, yet a little defiant. Then standing still and looking remotely ahead, she offered herself to the room. She was tiny, almost fragile in very high heels, a brown sheath dress, a brown fur cape, and a beaded toque on the back of her head.

Laura beheld her and a shudder passed through her, as if she recaptured a moment of Jamie. A moment of a Jamie she had never known. Then on an indrawn, trembling breath, she accepted her as a girl that he once had loved.

She rose and went forward. And then it was she who must bear the gaze. She smiled into it, her eyes gone blind.

"Michèle?" she said. "I am Laura Kendall." And their hands touched briefly; for no more than a moment, but it shocked them both. For each of them it was touching Jamie.

But after that, he was quite withdrawn. When they looked into one another's eyes, it was to each as if Jamie had never known the other. And they felt it was so with a deep surprise. Surely there was to be more than this . . .

And Laura said, "I am glad to see you." The face before her was flowerlike, pretty, with a certain fixed pertness about the lips. The chin was rounded and softly young. But the eyes were artful, very dark and carefully shadowed and penciled. And in their depths was an artfulness too, a kind of shrewdness. A distance, a judgment. Laura thought with wonder: her eyes are old. And she sickened a little, for it might be that Jamie had made them old.

She stood for a long and painful moment, wondering if she were to bear a guilt; on her son's behalf, accepting it gladly, if it must be so. But she could not tell. She was strangely lost.

She smiled and gestured toward the dining room beyond. Then she turned and led the way. She could hear the tap of the needle heels. There was an aura of perfume, subtle and expensive. Her mind cried out against finding this stranger. Finding Jean was as natural as finding her own face in the mirror before her. He belonged to be found. But this . . .

She did not look up again till they were seated, with menus. "Jean tells me," she said, "that you do not speak English." She waited then, and Michèle drew her eyes from the menu slowly and gave her a distant, speculative smile. "English?" Laura said.

Michèle shook her head. Her eyes strayed deliberately about the room. Nothing seemed to touch her. She was like a bit of porcelain, which in a certain corner in a certain light will have a look of life. It is because she can not understand me, Laura reasoned. But watching her; she felt a stir of formless panic. This girl, this woman, could dispose of Jean. And therefore she could dispose of Laura, too.

For it was deeply clear to Laura Kendall that the rest of her life depended on this hour.

Beyond the waiter, she could see Mrs. Carstairs watching them over the rim of her beer. Laura suddenly regretted telling her nothing. It would be good to know her an ally now.

Michèle ordered in French, her voice deliberate. It suggested assurance. Underneath, there was an echo of something like defiance. But of course, Laura thought. For her too, I am the enemy. As I am for all who love Jean and would keep him . . .

While they waited for food, the silence between them was a crystal thing, cool and hard-surfaced. They studied discreetly the uniform tables, white-covered and each with its bright, neat flowers; the bits of pewter arranged on the mantel above the hearth. All of it struck their crystal silence and seemed to be caught and reflected there. Laura grew aware of a feeling of shock, because there was nothing but this brittle silence. She could feel no movement; not even of envy that this girl had known and touched Jamie last. Only shock that a stranger was here before her. An alien face that her son had loved. . .

It began to be like a denial of Jamie that she could not shatter this crystal silence that was more than silence . . . that was almost a clearly spoken "no" between them.

She lowered her eyes to her hands on the table and held in her mind the face of Jean. When she raised them at last she caught the eyes of Michèle on herself. They were cautious, appraising. She had a sudden intuition that Michèle after all understood a little English.

When the waiter had served them and finally retreated, she tried to smile warmly at the face before her. Like a flower, it was, but almost waxen. By contrast, the dark hair was soft and fluid. The eyes were remote but vaguely watchful. The throat, bound with pearls, was supple and fragile as if by design. The narrow shoulders, strangely, were like a child's. Laura spoke slowly. "It is good of you to make the trip from Paris to see me . . . Your father tells me that you work in Paris, but he did not tell me what work you do."

She paused and waited. There was no reply. But she carefully did not seem to require one. She accepted the alert, listening gaze of Michèle. "I suppose," she said, "that your father has told you why I am here . . . and what I hope for." She looked away briefly and back again. "I hope to take Jean for a little while."

She picked up her glass of the pale, light beer and put it down abruptly. Her hand was trembling, and Michèle had noticed. She drew her hands away to her lap and folded them. Michèle had begun to eat thoughtfully, delicately. "Of course . . . Of course, you are the one to say. To say if I may have him for a little while."

There was no indication that her words were understood. Across the room, Mrs. Carstairs was watching from behind an after-dinner cloud of smoke. She had an air of having heard more than Michèle.

Laura said at last, her voice low, "I can not tell you how wonderful it is that I should find him . . . find Jean. It's like a miracle. I can not tell you. And even if I can not have him . . . Believe me, I know what I ask. I ask a very great thing . . ." She paused for a moment, because the face before her was so terribly remote. "Even if I can't . . . still, to know he is found, he is here . . . Born. Alive. I wish I could tell you." She had not intended this. The words had come, and they brought a strange relief. "I am alone in the world. And suddenly I am not. Not alone. If I could explain it, you would know that I thank you."

The waiter was beside her. "Madame, is not good? Something?"

She looked up at him, uncertain, unable to reply. She found that she was trembling. "Oh, yes," she said finally. "I'm not hungry, that is all."

He hovered about them, with his waiter's concern, limping a little, as it pleased him to do. And when Michèle put down her fork, he leapt to them. Removing the plates, he seemed to gather Laura's words and bear them away with her uneaten food.

Anyway, I have said it. I have said it, she thought. Michèle gave a little sigh and sipped her beer, her fingers surrounding it, delicate and pale, with very pink nails. There was an opal ring. There was something detached and contained in her gesture.

Laura sat smiling, her mind dismayed. "Perhaps you would talk to me. In French, of course."

Michèle looked at her, half frowning, a line of calculation between her brows. Then she smiled very briefly and gazed around the room. She took out her cigarettes and offered them to Laura.

Laura shook her head. She watched Michèle light one,

139

watched the curl of smoke cloud the fragile face. She felt that
Michèle had understood her a little, and that she was waiting.
But waiting for what? She saw, for the first time, that Jean did
not resemble her; no more, indeed, that he resembled Jamie.

When the waiter returned with two stemmed glasses of a
pale green ice, she said to him calmly: "*Garçon*, the young
lady speaks only French."

He glanced swiftly around.

"No, the lady here with me. Will you tell her something?
Tell her that after we have finished with dinner, I should like
her to come upstairs to my room."

He bowed very gravely and shifted his towel. He addressed
Michèle, who listened, her face expressionless. She nodded
when he had finished. Then she stubbed out her cigarette and
spoke to him, briefly, her eyes on the table.

"Madame, she is ready to go quickly at once."

"Thank you," said Laura. "Then I think we shall go."

She rose, while he looked at them with reproach. He swept
the ices back onto the tray and retreated slowly, overcome with
limping.

They climbed the stair in silence. In the bedroom Laura
turned to Michèle. "Please sit here." She touched the large,
flowered chair by the window.

Michèle looked around her with a swift, appraising glance.
She hesitated; then she walked to the chair and sat down.

"There is something," Laura said, "that I wanted you to
have." She turned rather blindly to the closet and got down her
dressing case from the shelf. She placed it on the dresser and
opened it. Inside, behind the mirror, was the picture of Jamie,
but she did not reach for it. She took out instead a small parcel,
tissue-covered, and carefully unfolded it. Then she held up the
contents. It was a modest ornament; a blue stone rimmed with
silver, and a silver chain. Her hands trembled as she held it.

The eyes of Michèle were alert and appraising.

"It was in a box of things that Jamie sent home just before he was killed. He had bought them somewhere over here. Opera glasses, a camera, and some other things. He didn't say who they were for. They just came. I suppose he wanted later to give them to people . . . When I knew he wasn't coming back, I opened them, you see. And I thought . . . I thought you might like to have this to keep." In a kind of despair, she made the useless explanation, hoping that her voice would convey the thought.

The eyes of Michèlle were on the shimmering pendant.

"Jamie," Laura said, and placed it in her hand.

Michèle, without expression, looked at it in her open palm. She seemed to be uncertain as to what she would do.

"Jamie," Laura said, her voice close to breaking. "I wish you to have it. It is yours, if you like." She looked down through a mist upon the dark, shining hair, richly, softly waving about the edges of the toque. And the faint breath of perfume seemed to rise from the stone in the open palm.

If only she would speak to me, Laura thought. If she would speak to me in French, it would be better than nothing. But this silent receiving of her son's possession! It was as if he lay in the open hand; and not really received, only suffered to remain.

She turned in desperation and returned to the dressing case. From behind the little mirror she took the picture of Jamie. She looked at it first, before she showed it to the girl.

"Do you have one?" she asked. "Would you like to have this?"

Michèle did not move. She stared at the picture through her darkened lashes. It was a stare of curiosity, of memory and indifference, that suddenly flickered with a small impatience.

She never loved him, Laura thought with shock. Or if she loved him, it was not for long.

She turned away with the picture. Her mind was dead. She walked to the window and back to the dressing case and put away the picture. When she shut the case, it seemed to her that she loved Jamie more than she had ever done. And she loved his son more. She wanted Jean forever. She longed to take him from this place where his father was not loved.

The telephone startled her. She picked it up. It was Marc Duriez at the desk in the lobby. He asked if Michèle were with her.

"Yes," she said faintly, relieved to hear his voice. "She is with me now."

"You will tell her that I wait, if you please."

Before she could reply, she saw that Michèle was standing beside her and was holding out her hand for the phone, with a smile. Michèle spoke into it in a rapid French. She handed it back to Laura with another smile.

When Laura took the phone, Marc Duriez had hung up. She put it down slowly.

Michèle had walked away to the window and was moving before it, looking down at the garden. She has grace, Laura thought. She was acutely aware of the girl's fluid movement, as if in herself she felt a painful echo. She dances, perhaps.

Laura looked at the desk across the room. In the drawer was paper and a pen and ink. With a kind of weariness, still watching the girl, she told herself that in a moment she would go to the desk and take out the paper and write her request. She would ask her simply and humbly for Jean, and later Marc Duriez would put the words into French.

But she had not yet moved, when he knocked on the door. When she opened it, she saw at once that Michèle had asked him to come. Laura stood aside. "We need you," she said. And she wanted again simply to touch his hand.

"Is it so?" he said gravely and entered the room.

Michèle had come to meet him. She spoke to him briefly. He answered with a word.

"Please sit down," Laura said and indicated the chairs. She went herself and sat on the foot of the bed. But he stood by the door just inside the room, the brown trench coat unbuttoned, hanging loose. There was a grayness in his face. The lines from mouth to chin were deeper, she thought. His eyes on Michèle were narrowed and dark with a weariness that troubled her.

"You're tired," she said, unconscious of her words. He glanced at her so deeply, so remotely that she was startled and subdued. He seemed to have known her all the years of her life and to look at her, remembering the way she had been.

She said, without taking her eyes from his face, "Michèle can not understand me . . ."

He made no sign.

"Have you told her?" she asked.

"I have told her," he said.

She wanted suddenly to stop the words that would come into the room, but she wanted it too late. "What does she say?"

He turned his eyes to Michèle. "She has not given to me the answer."

She said to him slowly. "Will you ask her for me now?" And something deep inside her cried out against herself, that she should force him to turn and ask his daughter this thing.

He did not speak at once. "What is it you wish to say to her?" he said finally.

She looked away. Her voice was low. "Say that I wish to take Jean to America for a while. Say that I want him for the rest of the school year. And in the summer . . . next summer . . . I shall bring him back."

She waited. She was trembling. In that moment, she understood how bizarre was her request, how impossible to grant. It defied all reason . . . all humanity, as well.

Michèle was poised and tense, with a listening face. And suddenly she drew the fur cape from her shoulders and threw it on the chair with a swift, deliberate motion. She spoke a fierce, impatient word to her father.

He looked at her levelly. His mouth was strange. In a moment, he spoke in French. She listened, her chin lowered, her eyes staring upward.

When he had finished, she did not move. She darted a rapid glance at Laura, and back. Slowly she raised her head and spoke, her voice rising.

He watched her, motionless. He did not speak. But he reached out and touched the wall behind him with his hand.

Michèle spoke again and turned away to the window.

Laura listened, her heart pounding. She could not bear Marc Duriez's face, the vacancy that sought to hide the vivid anguish beneath. "If tomorrow would be better . . . I could call you tomorrow."

He did not seem to hear. He said to her at last, with his eyes on the floor. "My daughter wishes to say that you may take the boy."

She rose from the bed without awareness of her movement. She wanted to be sure that she had heard him right. "She says that I may take him to America?"

He nodded.

"When may I take him?"

"Now," he replied.

She could have covered her face; from joy or from sorrow, she did not know which.

144

Michèle, from the window, turned and spoke again. She took a cigarette from her purse and lit it. Then she moved from the window, and with a slow, defiant grace, she lifted her cape from the chair where it lay.

He closed his eyes against her.

Laura looked from him to Michèle, and back. And when she measured finally the distance between them, her heart was stunned; as if she stood in his place and felt the betrayal. She turned away her eyes. She could not see his defeat. It became too much her own. It became Jamie dying and the telegram that told it.

"But why?" she asked. She did not know her own voice. "Why does she want this?"

He shook his head.

"Ask her why?" she insisted, her words tense and low.

"She has said it. She has said there is a man, an older man, that she wishes to marry . . . and he does not wish the child."

"But you would keep the child . . ."

He looked at her, his face strained.

She repeated it. "You would keep him."

"I would keep him . . . of course. But this man wishes to be no danger that later the boy will come . . ." He spoke the word "danger" in a slow, clipped way, as if it were not a word but a phrase, a sharp command. "He would find my daughter more desirable if the boy is in America."

She looked away to the window. There was a hard sort of stillness behind her in the room that she could not bear. Beyond the curtain, the very air had a golden softness, and the garden below her rested for the moment in an amber, golden haze. Very rich and deep it looked, and blown and scattered, but held for the moment in this molten glory. She thought, looking down, This is the finest day . . .

And it was pain in her breast to find it like this, when behind

145

her the silence was leaden in the room. She thought all at once: I have made it this way. I have come across the world and I have made this silence.

I have made this silence between the father and his child.

She turned around slowly, with the pain in her eyes, I am taking what is left him. I am taking Jean. And she looked him full in his silent face. There was nothing in his face but a depth of silence. I am taking in my own hand what does not belong . . .

He said to her gently, "I think now we go . . ." He turned away. "Later . . . later we speak."

She could not answer him or make a sign. Michèle was smoking quietly, her little fur cape caught onto one arm. She seemed detached and prepared to leave.

He moved to the door and opened it and turned. He gazed for a long moment back at Michèle. He drew his glance slowly and finally to Laura. She could not read his face.

"Madame," he said at last, "it is my daughter's . . . position," he spoke the word carefully, "that there has been in the past little that is of satisfaction in her life. It is difficult for me not to agree that it is so. I believe," he said slowly, "you would agree with her too."

She did not reply.

"And therefore, madame, you will not too much condemn her for arranging her happiness . . . when you have kindly offered her the means to arrange it."

He looked beyond her at the room with a smiling blindness. "If one could say that your son has been to blame . . . in some little way . . . to some extent, that is . . . ," he paused for a moment, "then you, madame, are making his forgiveness. You are making him right, is it so? When you give it to her to have her life in the way that she wishes."

It seemed to her that he spoke with the bitterest of irony in

146

the moment that he pled the defense of his child. She was stunned, and a wild, confused shame overwhelmed her. It came to her suddenly that if Jamie were to blame—though she could not grant it, but if he were to blame, then she took up his guilt. And she did not wipe it out, she increased it tenfold. In spite of his words, she saw it in the face of the man before her, that she did not wipe it out but increased it tenfold.

And then far back in his eyes she discovered the hushed, the pained, the almost tender regret that it must be she who was the means of his hurt. The hour they had passed in the farmhouse was there. And she saw that in that hour, while he sat with his eyes on the bird overhead, he had given it into her waiting hands to make this later hour when she stripped him of much.

She said to him then, "Could it be for one month? Or for two or three? I see that perhaps I have asked too much."

He studied her for a while, his mouth fixed in a smile. "She wishes that you keep the boy for some time in your country . . . She wishes that you agree before you shall take him."

She turned away then. She could not watch them leave.

When she heard the door close, she looked up slowly and saw the blue pendant of Jamie's on the dresser. She picked it up and held it in her hand for some time. Then, clasping it tightly, she lay down on the bed.

THE TELEPHONE roused her. She looked at her watch, and it was almost four o'clock.

The voice was Mrs. Carstairs'. "I do hope I didn't wake you."

"No, I wasn't sleeping."

"Well, I've just put on the kettle. And my order has arrived, with a fresh tin of biscuits. I always feel selfish when I break the seal for me. Mrs. Kermit isn't coming. Her nap is longer on Sundays. It's the way she keeps the Sabbath . . . For myself, I only drop a little rum in my tea. The Major picked up the custom. And it quite restores Belief."

Laura could not bring herself to answer for a moment. "I really don't think so for today . . . but thank you."

"Not feeling well?"

"Not too well."

"Well, tea is what you need. I'll make it very weak." She sounded thoroughly convinced. She finished cheerfully, "I've found it always helps. Even in death." The enigmatic statement hung suspended in the air.

Laura heard it with a tremor of hysteria in her throat. But if there was a remedy that commanded such faith . . . She lay back weakly, the phone against her cheek. "All right," she said, "I'll come . . . It will take me a minute."

She lay still. In her mind was Mrs. Carstairs' face at dinner staring over her beer at Michèle and herself. She did not stir. Then she thought of the kettle now beginning to bubble, and how the water must be poured the very second it boiled. Then the tea leaves must steep for a full five minutes. And then it must be poured. . . .

It was enough to make her rise. Perhaps it was good to have it all so inflexible. When one's life goes slack . . . perhaps it is a mercy to have the tyranny of tea.

And of course it had always been a part of the ritual that in twenty minutes' time Laura Kendall would reveal that Jean Duriez was her grandson. It seemed so inevitable that she did not really struggle. Indeed, it brought a relief. She was grateful, for the moment, that there was some one in her world who would listen with interest. She did not tell it all; she confined the revelation to the simple fact of kinship. She could speak it with pride.

And of course, since she was human, and moreover a

woman, there remained the satisfaction of dropping the bomb-shell, of rendering another woman wholly speechless with a word.

She felt oddly better to have summed it up: "Jean Duriez is my grandson." It was all that ever mattered. Whatever fol-lowed must pale before that fine, clear fact.

Already, almost, she had made her decision.

III

SHE GAVE her name to the self-possessed woman at the desk. The latter began in the voice of efficiency, "You are a former patient?" But she recognized the face, or perhaps the name. She clutched at the drawer of the cabinet behind her.

"I was here last week."

Then the woman was eyeing the blank card with suspicion. There was nothing but the name and the name of the inn.

"I should like to be the last to see the doctor."

The woman was alert.

"When everyone has gone, I should like to see him then." And at once Laura read in the face before her how it sometimes happened that the celebrated charm of Dr. Duriez was sufficient to produce in the ladies of the inn a few symptoms not easily detailed on a card.

Laura met her eyes coldly. "I shall wait," she said. And she turned with frank anger to sit with the rest. She closed herself away from the movement of the room. For some time, she watched from the window the walnut tree the children had shaken with laughter. The yard was now deserted. They are in school, she thought . . . Jean is in school. He has begun his life . . . The life she had given up trying to possess. She felt a strange relief because it was over. Or was it over? Perhaps Marc Duriez, out of pity, would suggest a way. Perhaps in another year, or two or three . . . But of course it must be less than she had dared to dream. She was almost stunned now to know the breadth of her dream.

She watched the patch of sky beyond the tree and the ramparts paling and pearling, growing thick and opal, then slowly kindling into chrome-like radiance. No sun anywhere, but the deepening radiance, heavy and molten, like a liquid thing, as warm and fluid as the children's laughter. She looked with amazement at their walnut tree. For it stood transfigured and drowned in light. Not a yellowed leaf stirred or fell to the grass. Then slowly, with a current in the ocean of light, the branches were caught up and drifted a little. Rhythmically, gently, the leaves floated outward and down with the stream. Like the hair of a Rhine maiden lifting and falling in enchanted depths.

Then, while she watched, the light-drowned tree seemed haunted with the laughter of all its children, and of all her own. With Jamie's, and the children's on the lawn of the Abbaye, and with Jean's when he showed her the cat's-eye stone.

And she could not breathe, because she had outlived all her children. She had lost them all in what was called a past.

Her heart contracted when she heard her name. She rose and went into Marc Duriez's room.

He stood when he saw her. "Madame," he said. And then, "Please to sit." His voice was strange.

She glanced with a little smile down at her watch. "It is time for your lunch, and I will not stay . . ." It was suddenly over, all but the telling. She was perfectly calm. "I came to say that I can not accept your daughter's decision. I find that I can not take Jean after all."

He stood quite still at the edge of his desk.

"This is done why?" he said at last, his accent so deep that she scarcely understood.

She looked at him fully. In another place, another house, a bird shuddered overhead, and she seemed to hold the heart of this bird in her hand. She glanced away. "I suppose I didn't think that I should really succeed. And now I have thought it over . . ." Her voice broke a little, but she smiled at the leather-bound books on his walls. "He is quite, quite safe with you. But I wanted to be sure."

"Madame, you will sit . . ." He said it sharply, with command in his voice.

She looked at him, surprised. "If you wish it," she answered. And she went and sat down in front of his desk.

He paced the length of the room. He picked up a volume from the top of his desk and replaced it carefully on a low wall shelf. When he rose again, his face was florid and enclosed. He swept his hand through the ends of his hair. He took his pipe from the desk and struck it against his gloved hand and laid it down.

She waited in a kind of suspension of living. She did not try to think. Somehow she had reached the top of her hill, and she rested a moment before starting down.

"This is done why?" He asked it again.

She looked at him, her face flushed and perplexed. She could not answer him for a moment. "I have told you, I think."

"I think you have not . . ." He turned away and then abruptly back. "I think it is so much not why it is done, that you could not tell it again, what was said."

She sighed and shook her head. "You are not very clear."

"It has not the exactness perhaps, but you know."

She began deliberately to consider the fact that the more susceptible ladies of the inn could hardly have seen him in difficult moods. She was thinking it to stop the tears in her throat.

"Please . . . ," she said suddenly. "I should like to go." But after all she did not make any move. She looked up into his absorbed gray eyes, and she thought that she would not forget, for as long as she lived, this strange and difficult and deeply unhappy man.

She smiled at him sadly, with a stir of impatience. "There is no need . . . I am giving you back everything that was yours. I am putting it all back, just as it was."

"It is impossible," he said, "to put it back as before."

"You are right, of course. But I am doing my best . . ." She looked away. "I should like you to tell Jean goodbye for me."

He stared at her angrily. "It is not so simple."

She turned to him wearily, with supplication. "Please . . . ," she said. "You are angry with me. Before, when perhaps I deserved it, I believe you were not. But now . . ."

"No, madame, I am not angry with you, as it pleases you to say. But I can not help telling you to leave is not simple."

She closed her eyes. "Tell me," she said, "what you want me to do."

He came and sat down behind his desk. He opened a drawer and closed it softly. When he looked up, she saw it in his eyes that he had reached an end of something and was searching out a way to begin again. "We will ask him to come here now," he said.

"Jean? But he will be in school."

"At this time for the meal he is being at home."

"I see. But I wouldn't call him. There is really no need

. . ." She gazed at him helplessly. "I am thinking of myself. I should find it easier . . ."

"No," he answered, "it will be in me a thing I can not sleep for at night."

He got up and went to the door and opened it. The waiting room was empty. The woman at the desk had gone away to eat. Then Laura heard him calling through the open door into the hall. She heard Jean's name.

When he returned, he was smiling, his eyes grim, oddly whimsical, a little like the eyes of her husband, who was dead, when he had shared with her the laughter at the heart of things. He was saying, "It will be like a bad novel. A very bad one. But we shall ask him to choose."

Her heart sprang outward in a kind of pain. She had outlived the delicate, ironic twist. She shook her head. "There is no reason for this. We know how he will choose . . . He will be right, of course. You have always been so careful to leave him undisturbed. Uninvolved in our . . ." She could not say the word. In a moment she asked it, "Are you doing this to punish me a little, perhaps?" She regretted it at once.

He turned to her as if she had struck him in the face. He sat down behind the desk. There was a brightness in his eyes. "Believe me, madame . . ."

He broke off. Jean was standing in the door.

He looked so small and so dishevelled, so bewildered and at once so much a little wiser than before, that she longed to ask him how his school had been. There was a lead pencil mark, like a scar, down his cheek. A thread of his sweater had begun to unravel. And she wanted to assure him that tomorrow would be easier. She could tell that he was hungry, and her heart accused her for delaying his lunch.

Marc Duriez began at once to speak to him in English in a

gentle voice. "Jean, you are old enough to know what it is that you like."

Jean spoke a puzzled phrase in French.

"No, we shall speak aloud the English so that the *grand-mère* may comprehend."

The boy looked at her, then nodded, his eyes wide and attentive.

"Now, Jean . . . the *grandmère* would like to take you to America. Your *maman* has said to me that you may go . . ." He waited for a little, his hand shielding his eyes. It struck her suddenly that she saw them for the first time together, and that underneath the quiet firmness of his tone, Marc Duriez was given into the hands of this child.

She looked away. In the depths of her mind she had always wondered if he found Jean a burden. Perhaps she had hoped it. But in his voice there was the grateful acceptance of a gift, of its being daily given and daily received. It is the only way to live with a child, she was thinking. It seemed to her that with Jamie she had not always known it, but that now, in this child, she might redeem herself.

It is the joy of a grandchild: you may redeem yourself.

Marc Duriez continued. "The *grandmère* says that in America there is the splendid school, *une école splendide*, where you may go for one year and live as the American boys live and learn to speak the English as the American boys speak it. And that would be very good. It would be a good thing not to grow up and have to heave and grumble through it as your *grandpère* does now."

After a moment he went on: "But that is not the great thing. It is a fact that the *grandmère* loves you and would like to have you being near to her, so that you may know her more and love her as much as she loves you." He paused and said in a low voice, "The *grandmère* is very sad . . . *très triste* . . . because her son died. That was your father. And because the other *grandpère* died, and now she has no one left but you."

"The other *grandpère*?" Jean asked.

"The other *grandpère* was married to this *grandmère*."

"He is dead?"

"That is right."

The boy looked silently from one to the other. As last he said, carefully, "It is that I have now one *grandpère* and one *grandmère*."

"That is right."

They were all silent. Marc Duriez sat with his head between his hands. At last he said, "You would like this?"

The boy did not reply.

"Is it that you would like to go with the *grandmère*?"

Laura spoke, her voice full. "You are not fair to yourself . . ."

He did not answer at once. "The boy knows," he said.

"But he may not," she answered. "He may be too young to know. Really know."

Still, he did not speak, but sat, his hands shielding his eyes.

Laura closed her own for a moment. Then she turned to the boy. "You must know, Jean, how much the *grandpère* loves you . . . and needs you to stay."

He withdrew his hands abruptly. "Madame . . ."

She rose and stood quietly before him. "I am going now."

He looked up at her. "Go, Jean," he said.

The boy gazed from one to the other.

"*Va, maintenant*," Marc Duriez said softly.

And Jean turned. They listened to the clatter of new shoes bought for school and as yet scarcely manageable, and then to the silence.

"That was not necessary," he said.

"But it was. You made it so." She tried to smile, but her lips were trembling.

He looked at her silently; he did not rise. For a moment, strangely, it seemed to her that they were not talking about Jean at all, but about something else; and what it was, she could not say. She dared not put the glance between them into any sort of words, lest she lose her way. She said carefully, "It is the boy and what is best. It is Jean, after all . . ."

"Yes," he said, stirring. "Sit down, if you please."

But she shook her head. He rose slowly. She said into his eyes, "I wanted something. I didn't think what I was doing . . ." She turned away. "But you are generous. You have understood. And I think you have forgiven." She turned back and held out her hand. She was smiling. "And now I have finished. I shall write him letters, if I may. It will be good for his English. And one year, before long . . . perhaps next year, who knows? . . . I shall come back to see him." She looked past his head. "It will be enough for me to know . . . that he is in the world . . . Tell me," she finished gaily, "what day he was born. I should like to send him something . . ." She broke off. He had not taken her hand.

"Madame," he said abruptly in a kind of desperation.

She waited, her eyes upon him. He said slowly, "You make of this a complexity."

Yet he had recently condemned her for making it simple.

"Do I?" she asked at last.

"Yes," he said. "Yet it is the so simple affair." His English was becoming awkward; his spirit was under stress.

He came from behind the desk and walked the length of the room. When he turned, he asked, "You will be staying in Montreuil for one long time?"

She watched him for a moment, wondering. Then she shook her head. "No, there is nothing more. I shall be leaving . . ."

"But when?"

"I hadn't thought. But tomorrow. I'll have to ask about the trains."

"Tomorrow," he said. "It is not . . . there is not the reason for tomorrow."

She watched him still, not sure of understanding.

He repeated it. "There is not the reason for tomorrow."

She said softly, "But I have finished here."

Almost angrily he looked at her. "But I have not finished."

They stared at one another across the length of the room. Almost enemies. No, almost something else, quite different, that she dared not see. His face went dark before her. She put her hand upon the chair. Then she saw it, but she denied it. At once, at once, while she could still command herself, while she could still deny. She thought, when you are forty-five, you are thinking underneath that time is running out, and you see things in a face that are not there. Things that hold back time . . .

Things that hold life.

He did not move. "There is not the reason that you leave this place."

"Leave Montreuil?"

He nodded. He went on gazing at her still, it seemed to her, with anger. "It is this language," he said fiercely. "It has not the words." His eyes besought her, helpless. "It is impossible in it the exactness . . . And if it has not the exactness, you leave Montreuil, it is so."

She looked at him. She fought to bring his words into focus. "I can not stay on without a reason, even to be with Jean."

"But yes. But it was not. It was in my mind another thing . . ." He abandoned speech abruptly.

"Shall I say it?" she asked at last, in answer to his appeal. He nodded, his face tense.

158

Her mind felt numb, as if she had been handed a part in a play and she needed more time to make the words sound real. She said slowly, "You are trying to tell me that we both want the same . . . that we both want the child . . ."

He was still, and then he nodded.

She looked away. She smiled briefly. "It is a little as Jean was saying: there is now one *grandpère* and one *grandmère* . . . You are offering me a marriage with yourself, so that we both may have him."

He looked at her, relieved and yet uncertain. "It is the way of my thinking . . ."

She said, "You believe this to be a reasonable solution."

"It has the reason in it, yes." He was watchful, reluctant.

She was smiling at him gravely. "But it lacks what? The exactness?"

He smiled back at her. "It lacks of you to be serious."

She laughed softly, taking his smile to remember . . . later, much later, for the rest of her life. "It lacks of you to be a little Paris." She sobered. "But I thank you. I thank you from the bottom of my heart. You are generous . . . more than that. I have never known . . ." She broke off and turned to the door.

"Laure . . ." He gave her name in French. It was the first time he had spoken it. She stopped quite still, as if his hand had held her. "I think it has not been said what is meant between us . . . what is here. You have taken words I can not know as well and made them into what I have not understood to mean."

She drew a long breath before she turned. Her eyes scanned the books on the walls, the desk, the frivolous quill pen, the photograph of Jean . . . as if she sought them for words. She said very quietly, "I think . . . I believe that something like this has happened." She could not look at his face. "Shall I tell you what I think?"

She was aware that he waited. In the distance, she seemed to hear the sound of Jean's voice.

"You have resented my son for seven years, and more. And there was no one to whom you could speak out against him. And I come. I am here. And it is good to tell me you have hated my son."

He made a gesture of protest.

She went on. "After you have said it, you are relieved of the bitterness. And you begin to warm to me, who have given you this relief . . . after seven years."

"No."

She looked at him then. "You wanted peace of mind . . . and I have brought you a little."

"No!" he said with violence. "You are wrong. You have made a complexity."

She waited for a moment. "You are very kind." She said it gently: "But is it not a little like this . . . bad novel of yours?"

She had known that would end it, and she walked through the door.

She drove to the inn in a deep confusion and yearning. I want too much, she whispered. I can not have it all again. Not the two things again . . . Not the two loves again. It isn't love he offers, but something else. Something less. If I stayed I could begin to ask for more than I am offered.

She would not let herself be broken once again in a lifetime.

Deliberately, she told herself to give them up. I can do it, she said. I have done it before. It takes the practice I have had. This time it will be easier, for I have done it before.

The rain had stopped and the air was translucent, cool and quite still. The pearl yellow sky seemed to wait in the stillness. Then faintly the wind woke in the tips of the trees, and shuddered down the orange flame bodies of the poplars, and settled in the hedges where it tossed and sighed.

She left the car in the garage and walked across the cobblestones. In the clean, moving air, the two she had found in this place became in her memory one unspeakable gift, that was given her for an hour. She had thought to make them separate, and to keep the child for longer. But she saw it clearly now, how together they were given, and could not be divided, but together must be taken and together given back . . . at the hour's end.

Walking through the iron gate, she gave them back.

Yet her own voice whispered: What am I to do with all the hours that are left? And to answer it, she remembered the trip with Mrs. Carstairs. The drive to Merlimont they had talked of on occasion. She tried to think of it with pleasure. She tried to want a glimpse of the coast and the Channel before she left here tomorrow.

She stopped at the desk and made arrangements for a train on the following morning. "Ah, madame," the desk clerk said, "we had hoped it would arrange the mind of madame to stay, the fine look of the country."

She smiled at him. "I wish I could stay." And suddenly the simple statement was almost a cry. She turned away quickly and went up the stairs.

When she reached her room, she picked up the telephone and asked for Mrs. Carstairs. "You know," she said to her, "I think that after all I'd like to go to Merlimont."

The voice at the other end replied with a moan.

"Mrs. Carstairs . . . ?" said Laura. "Are you quite all right?"

"My god, no. I'm in the throes of this parasitic thing."

"Oh dear, I'll be right down . . . Have you called for the doctor?"

"Yes . . . yes."

"I'll be right there."

Laura slipped off her coat and ran a comb through her hair.

Mrs. Carstairs was groaning on the bedspread in a dressing gown. She sat up when Laura entered.

"No, please. Lie down again."

She dropped back with a moan.

Laura helped her to slide beneath the covers. Then she went into the bathroom and soaked a cloth in cold water and wrung it out. There was a strong smell of tea. And the teapot on the shelf above the tub had a chip in its spout.

She summoned her sympathy. Indeed her mind knew compassion, but deep in her heart she was numb and unfeeling. To walk away from Marc Duriez with rejection on her lips, she must deny herself. She must plunge into the strange, cold waters of indifference. It frightened her to know how little she was moved. She returned and placed the cloth on Mrs. Carstairs' head. "Shall I call the desk about the doctor?"

"No, no, I called . . . When the bowl of ice arrives, explain to them it isn't wanted."

Between her pains, Mrs. Carstairs was alert, and even exhilarated. She half raised herself on the pillows. "It brings back the Major so . . . He was never more himself than in one of these attacks. The dreadful words he used, half English, half Indian. All terrible, terrible oaths that he saved for the occasion. The disease was so rare, he felt it called for something special . . ."

Pain bit off her words. "Henry . . . Henry," she murmured. When it was over, she smiled faintly at Laura. She went on sensibly, "The oaths I can remember have never seemed to help. Neither God nor the devil has ever been concerned with this particular trouble." She wiped her mouth with a handkerchief. "I have found it more helpful to call on the Major."

She was stricken for a moment. She continued presently, "After all, if the Major is somewhere—and believe me, my dear, at such times I can feel him very close. I tell you this to comfort you in your own situation—I'm sure he is regretting for my sake having eaten that half-baked goat in Tibet. It was a goat, you know. Not one of those cashmeres, but something very similar. A long-haired thing. The Major felt they would have rivalled the cashmeres for the sweaters. Except for this parasite which lays them low, you understand."

"Is there nothing you can do?" Laura asked. "No cure?"

"Nothing," the lady assured her on a rising note of triumph. "The Major, when he passed away, was written up in *The Lancet*. And I," she confided, "have left my body to be studied . . ." She paused to be stricken. ". . . which will be very soon. Very soon," she sighed.

She lay perfectly still, as if she were asleep. Laura went into the bathroom for another wet cloth. And when she laid it carefully, replacing the other, on Mrs. Carstairs' brow, the lady murmured easily, "I always feel like the toreador . . . his moment of truth."

"You mustn't try to talk."

"Otherwise, I couldn't say this . . ." She opened her eyes on Laura. "You have a little secret . . . Something you came for."

"Yes. But I've finished."

"What a pity, what a pity." She closed her eyes again and lapsed into silence. Then she said very clearly, "Nothing is ever finished."

Laura turned away, as if she would escape from the meaning of the words. If nothing is ever finished, I can't bear it, she thought.

She walked to the window. Surely when you lose, it is finished, she thought. Or do you go on losing for the rest of your life?

There was a knock at the door.

163

"It's the ice," said Mrs. Carstairs, and sank again into pain.

But it was indeed the doctor. Laura braced herself to face him. He stood in the hallway with his satchel in his hand. Not startled, she thought, but almost as if he had expected her to be there. As if this last encounter had been arranged from the beginning.

She stood aside for him to enter. Only his eyes acknowledged her. They went past her slowly to the woman on the bed. "Good day, madame," he said to Mrs. Carstairs, and walked into the room.

"Good day, doctor," said Mrs. Carstairs firmly, with all the pride of her disease, confident that in this quarter she could interest even more than if her face and form were lovely . . . and that deep within her battered body lay the power to baffle.

She sank into pain and rose from it, gasping. "My dear," she said to Laura, with a little note of cheer, "don't come back. Take your little trip. The doctor here will put me to sleep when he has finished."

"I shall wait and see," Laura said, her voice low in his presence.

"No, no, you mustn't miss it. I won't have it. I shall be all right." I shall have the good doctor to myself, she seemed to say. She lay back in exhaustion, closing her eyes. She was smiling faintly. A muscle in her throat moved slowly and relaxed.

Marc Duriez, leaning down, laid his hand on her forehead. With the gesture Laura knew her own compassion released. The weariness after pain came suddenly through his hand and into herself. As if only through Marc Duriez could she encounter other lives. But this is true, she thought with shock. This has become for me the truth. And she knew that when she left him, she would somehow be deprived. Deprived of some communion. Deprived of the fullness. Left alone with her own pain and loneliness forever.

She dared not look into his face. But when he took the hand of the suffering woman, it was as if he took her own to soothe her and heal her . . .

To bring her back into life . . . The clock by the bed sounded clearer and deeper. All the sky beyond the window was suddenly held luminous in the drinking glass beside it. And when the pale curtain stirred and crossed it with a shadow, there seemed to her such depths of tenderness in the world that she could not bear it and turned and left the room.

When she reached her own room, she got her suitcase from the top of the closet and began to pack it slowly. She folded her clothes carefully as if it were important, as if they must look well for another dozen countries. She tried not to think that after this there was the plane going home . . . Going home. To a place called home, where she had buried her dead.

But she could not finish and sat abruptly on the bed. After a while she lay down.

She lay still, thinking: I have loved a good man, and been loved by him. I have had one child, well made and all that I could ask for. It is more than many women have been given. Why should I look for more? And she embraced, in turn, her gifts and losses. Once more she took her grief into herself.

But as she lay detached and drifting out of time and space, and waiting till again that something out of darkness reached to her in love . . . suddenly her faltering heart was answering; faintly at first, and then more strongly, till the door inside burst open and she walked abroad in the world, as she had used to walk. Her mind drew breath in the windy plains of Artois. The eyes of her mind could find the sea beyond them. The voice of her mind was whispering words she had half forgotten. Till she lay shaken half in joy and half in pain; and all aghast, now wondering, now stern, and now indulgent, to know how swiftly she could turn from death to life . . .

It is my heart, she guessed, that can not break the habit of loving.

And then for one long moment, that she told herself must last her for a lifetime, she let herself behold him in the midst of her love. It was a way of knowledge. For as she saw him at a little distance, his face caught up into a clear light from her own, she searched him out and knew him, deeply, humbly, tenderly . . . all but became him, for his way became her way.

She smiled to think how sure the young could be—how sure she had herself been long ago—that they know all there is of loving.

Then she rose quietly and pulled aside the curtains from the windows. The leaves were all translucent with the hidden sun. She combed her hair and slipped into her coat. It seemed to her that if she stayed, she would be waiting for a word from him. Or perhaps she did not want to know that there would be no word, no knock, no call from the desk.

For there can be nothing else, she told herself as she went down the stairs. She did not stop at the desk to ask for the car, but went straight out and through the gate and across the cobblestones to the garage. She was thinking that when she returned she would call and say goodbye to Jean. But she must say it well and lightly, as if another year would be tomorrow.

On the way, the drops began to dapple her windshield. The wind was whipping up the tops of the trees. The dark blue hedges lay sodden by the roadside. The tower tops of wheat were muted gold in the rain. A city of golden towers on the naked plain.

She felt enclosed and alone in the little car, and sad, as if it were her own land she were leaving; and yet alive, as she had not been alive in years. Her mind went sweeping backwards, mistress of the past. No longer did she hear it whispered: that this happened . . . and then this happened. For she had found the child, and somehow that had stopped all sequence. The child had given her a place to stand.

The fields were drenched and open to the wind and rain. The earth and sky seemed washed and clean, aware of her, and merciful. As if they had known her from across the sea and waited for her all the years, with healing mercy in the running streams, the moving trees, the patterned rhythm of the harvest wheat.

And suddenly she had outrun the rain. Ahead of her, the sky was clear. And then the gray sea sprang like the wing of a gull between the sand dunes.

She parked in the low beach grass beside the road. She wound a scarf from the pocket of her coat about her hair. She got out and walked to the edge of the beach, then took off her shoes at the foot of a dune and climbed, falling breathless at the top in the cool wet sand. The wind came clean and cold against her, whipping the scarf against her eyes, holding her blind to what lay beyond. With the shock of the wind, and the feel of the sand against her palms, for an instant she was a child again . . .

Slowly she drew the scarf from her face. She stood up then and looked at the sea, letting her mind be swept of desire. Surely there must be a way to the spirit that blesses the past and desires nothing. And here with the sea she could almost find it . . . The wind made shadows across the water. A clean-washed loneliness lay on the shore. From the depths of the sand the day itself sprang luminous, pale. Far off, the lilac-gray shore and the sea were merged and haunted by a ghost of sky.

To bless the past and desire nothing.

She turned for a reason she could not tell. And he was behind her, below on the road. He was looking up, head bare, his cropped gray hair alive in the wind, his bulking brown trench coat streaked with rain.

She stood for a long moment, bracing herself. When she started down, he picked up her shoes at the foot of the dune and held out his hand to steady her descent. His face was grave. Without a word, he stooped and extended her shoes.

When she put out her foot, it was trembling. She tried to smile. "I know you are thinking I am old for this."

He straightened before replying. "Your feet are wet." She scarcely heard him for the wind. "I think you should get in my car, and I shall turn on the heater."

She followed him obediently. When the door had closed them in, the sound of the motor shut away the wind. They sat without speaking, without looking at one another. She took the scarf from her hair and folded it carefully and put it away in the pocket of her coat.

At last he said quietly, "Madame Carstairs told me where it is you would be going."

"Is she quite all right?"

"Yes. For the present."

"I think I should have waited to see how she would be."

He did not answer. He spread his hands on the steering wheel before him, then gripped it tightly. He said, "I have forty-eight years . . ." He seemed to brace himself against the slight vibration of the car. "No," he shook his head, "it is not the way."

He turned to her suddenly, his face tense, his eyes dark. "It is the language," he said.

She nodded slowly.

"Help me," he said.

She looked at him long and deeply.

"How help you?" she asked.

He held her eyes. "Say it the way it would be for you to stay."

She looked across the sand to the sea and shook her head. She forced her voice to be steady. "It has been one week. One week."

"It means?" he said at last.

"It's not enough."

"It means . . . it makes the reason that you stay till enough." He turned away abruptly. "We are not the children that we wait to grow up. To understand what we desire."

She began at last slowly, "You are French. I am American . . ." She turned to him. "For my son and your daughter it did not go so well . . . You have said it isn't possible . . ."

"They were children," he broke in. "They did not know, they did not try." And after a long moment, "It needs that we shall finish what it is they began."

She put her head back on the seat and closed her eyes. She said desperately, "I am trying to think if it will be good for Jean."

He answered her gravely. "I think it would be good for Jean."

"You think that? How do you mean?" She was aware that she was quietly pleading.

He nodded and paused, with his eyes upon her face. "I have not for him the *gaiété*. The light. You have said so."

"I have said . . . I thought that once you had it more. But that is not to say . . ."

He was nodding again. "It is in you . . . more."

She shook her head. "I have lost it."

"No," he answered. "I feel in you so much of this thing of which we speak."

She said, "You bring it out in me. It is only with you . . ." She stopped and turned her head.

He raised his hand deliberately and touched her hair. "I do not think of the boy. I do not think of him for days."

His hand was trembling on her face, and she closed her eyes. He went on. "I am thinking always that it can not be another way. It must be this way. When I try to think of how . . . when you have gone . . . I can not see it that way . . . I go blind in my mind. It is like it is with me in Chalosse when the sun is too much and the dark grows inside me to fight against the sun . . ."

His speech had lapsed into the deeper accent that marked his weariness, or his happiness. He said, "When we have married, I shall not speak this language for one week. I shall be at rest from it for one week."

She looked up at him through tears. "It is possible that I could learn to speak French."

He studied her doubtfully.

"Jean would teach me," she said.

"It is of no exact importance. It is not necessary to speak."

"But it is!" she cried out. "There is so much to say . . ."

She had only to find the words that were his. She was a child on the threshold of speech. She could not wait to begin.